Grief wei

Cameron's late w
and the pain of heading home to an empty house
still ate at him.

Is that going to change anytime soon, Lord?

The elevator inched to a halt, and the doors
whispered open. The outside world beyond
the long wall of lobby windows was dark,
and he hated the thought of going out in it.

Then he saw Kendra through a glass partition
in the far wall. The overhead light haloed her
golden hair and caressed her creamy complexion.
She looked so lovely.

Cameron supposed it was loneliness that made
him look. He missed a woman's soft and gentle
presence in his life. He'd glimpsed plenty of
women over the years, but not one of them made
him feel as if the world had simply melted away
until there was only her.

Kendra didn't know he was watching as she
leaned against the counter, turning to talk to her
sister. She sparkled, laughing, tilting back her
head to study the array of cheerful balloons
floating just out of reach.

Looking heavenward, he couldn't help thinking
the good Lord had just given him his answer....

Books by Jillian Hart

Love Inspired

Heaven Sent #143
*His Hometown Girl #180
A Love Worth Waiting For #203
Heaven Knows #212
*The Sweetest Gift #243
*Heart and Soul #251
*Almost Heaven #260

*The McKaslin Clan

JILLIAN HART

makes her home in Washington State, where she has lived most of her life. When Jillian is not hard at work on her next story, she loves to read, go to lunch with her friends and spend quiet evenings with her family.

ALMOST HEAVEN

JILLIAN HART

Love Inspired

Published by Steeple Hill Books™

STEEPLE HILL BOOKS

Steeple
Hill®

ISBN 0-373-87270-4

ALMOST HEAVEN

www.SteepleHill.com

Printed in U.S.A.

Love never gives up, never loses faith, is always hopeful, and endures through every circumstance.
—*Corinthians* 13:7

Chapter One

It had been a long, hot day. Exhaustion dulled the edges of Kendra's vision, but the familiar sight of her hometown fortified her, as it always did. The green of a well-kept park. The neat line of railroad tracks on one side of the main street and the tidy row of old-fashioned buildings on the other. The cheerful awnings of businesses. The friendly neon sign of her family's coffee shop still burned a bright blue and green in the front window.

She glanced at the clock on the dashboard—thirty-four minutes past four. Maybe she'd stop and beg for food and drink so she wouldn't have to find something in her practically empty cupboards at home. There was probably a box of her beloved macaroni and cheese, but she lacked the energy and the will to make it.

The brief blast of a siren startled her and she glanced in her side-view mirror. Sure enough, there was a patrol car behind her. Was she speeding? No, the speedometer's needle was a hair past twenty. If anything she was going too slow.

Maybe the sheriff needed to go around her. Well, she was towing a full four-horse trailer. There was no oncoming traffic. Couldn't he just pass her?

No, he stayed stubbornly behind her, not looking as if he intended to pass. That must mean he wanted her.

What did she do? Too many cars were parked along the street, so she signaled and crossed the yellow lines to the other side of the road. She hoped that wasn't illegal or anything, but it wasn't as if she had a choice.

The patrol car followed her over, lights flashing. Brace yourself, Kendra, here he comes.

The town sheriff stalked toward her. Gun on one hip, his powerful arms held to his sides, he walked with an athlete's strength and confidence.

Cameron Durango. One of the last men she wanted to be alone with in the universe. Had he always looked this good in his uniform? Why hadn't she noticed that before?

She was staring at him! And he was likely to notice that. What was wrong with her? She'd given up putting her faith in men a long time ago. It was a done deal, signed, sealed and delivered. A life decision she'd made, and that was that.

The *last* thing she should be noticing was how striking Cameron looked in his uniform. Get a grip, Kendra. He's the sheriff. Nothing more. Nothing less. He arrests people. He pulls over perfectly innocent drivers for no reason at all.

His boots crunched in the gravel beside her pickup.

Don't look at him. "I wasn't speeding."

"Hey, Kendra." He whipped off his hat and the breeze ruffled the dark ends of his military short hair. "How are you doing this fine summer's day?"

"Hot."

"Yeah? A fine rig like this ought to have air-conditioning standard, right?"

"Sure, but I'm pulling a full load. I don't want to overheat the engine."

"I understand. I'd baby a new truck if I had one. You got this, what, a month ago?"

She stared straight ahead, not wanting to answer. Okay, she wasn't rude by nature and she felt lame acting that way. But Cameron Durango knew something about her that nobody else did, not even her sisters.

It didn't matter how fine he looked or how friendly he seemed, he reminded her of things best left forgotten.

Couldn't he just go?

"Yeah," she finally said. "That's why I haven't been driving around the truck I used to have, the one that kept breaking down on me."

"Right." Maybe he got the hint, because he paused, as if debating what to do next. Did he leave? No. He rested his forearms on the door of her truck. "Bet you're wondering what you did wrong to get me on your tail?''

"No. I wasn't speeding.'' Maybe if she was difficult, he'd leave her alone. Ticket her or whatever he was going to do and be on his way. So she wouldn't have to remember.

"I was sitting in the shade in my air-conditioning, tucked behind the Town Welcomes You sign, hoping to catch a hoard of speeding tourists and boost the town's income, when you meander along, driving responsibly and under the limit.''

"You admit it.''

"I noticed you were about to lose a tire on your trailer and decided to leave my shady spot behind to come warn you.''

Was he trying to be friendly? And it bugged her because she didn't want to like him. It would be way easier if he was going to unjustly ticket her, instead of help her.

She didn't need his or any man's assistance. "I've got doubles.''

"Still, you're carrying a heavy load.''

"I checked all the tires before I left the auction.'' He was right, and she realized the same thing herself, but was she going to tell him that? No. "Which tire?''

"Back right. Wouldn't want you to have a blowout or anything. You could get hurt.''

He had kind eyes, dark and deep, and a rugged face. Not classically handsome but chiseled as if made from granite. He had a straight blade of a nose, an uncompromising mouth and a square jaw that gave him an air of integrity.

If he were mean, it would have been much easier not to like him. But he wasn't. The worst thing about Cameron Durango was that he was a decent guy. He may carry a gun on his hip and look powerful enough to take down a two-hundred-pound criminal with a body blow, but he had a good heart.

Not that you could tell it from the outside.

Don't think about that night. Cold snaked through her veins, where her heart used to be. If there had been anything redeeming about that horrible night when everything changed for her, it was Cameron's kindness. He'd been truly kind, when she'd neither wanted it nor needed it.

Remembering, she couldn't meet his gaze. Staring hard at the steering wheel, she ran her fingertip around the bottom of the rim. Since that night she hadn't wanted to be alone with any man. Especially Cameron.

"I'll get that changed. Thanks for letting me know. It was decent of you."

"I try to be decent when I can. Especially to a pretty lady like you."

The way he said it wasn't flirtatious or anything, but he *was* sounding friendly. It made her start to shake.

She really wanted him to go. "Thanks again."

But he didn't leave. "Let me guess. You were at

the sale today. The Bureau of Land Management's auction.''

Was he trying to make small talk? It was probably a slow day for him. Hardly anyone was out and about in this heat, but still. She didn't know Cameron well and that's the way she wanted it. Could she be outright rude and tell him so? No.

''I saw the flier—it came to the office. You got wild mustangs back there?''

''Yes.''

She kept staring at her steering wheel. Icy sweat broke out on her palms. This was the way it was whenever she was alone with any man near her age.

Would it always be this way? Prayer had helped her; at least she didn't shake so hard that he might notice.

''Wow. Mind if I take a peek at them?''

Oh, so he was interested in the horses. Kendra relaxed a little but the quaking didn't stop. ''Sure. Just be careful. They're not used to people yet.''

''I'll just look.'' His grin was in his voice.

Kendra's gaze flashed to the side mirror where he was ambling away, his boots striking the dirt at the side of the road with a muffled rhythm.

With his spine straight and shoulders squared, he looked invincible. Undefeatable. Like everything honest and good and all-American. Just as he'd been for her, a calm strength when the world was smashing apart around her.

Get a grip, Kendra. That night was a long time ago.

It isn't worth thinking about. Jerrod was gone and a part of the past. Look forward, not back.

Cameron crunched through the gravel as he returned. "Those are some fine-looking animals you got."

"Thanks." She appreciated Cameron's help, but now she knew about the tire. She would fix it and be on her way—once he was on his. "I don't want to hold you up. I know you have speeders to catch and tickets to write."

"Are you trying to get rid of me?"

Yes. "Here comes a car right now. You might need to check your radar. Could be income for the town."

He peered in the direction of the luxury sedan creeping down the main street. "Mrs. Greenley? Nah, she's driving under the limit, like she always does. I've clocked her for the better part of the six years I've worked in this town and never caught her speeding once. The town is safe from rampaging, careless drivers for a few more seconds, it looks like."

"You can never be too sure. You go back to your speed trap and I'll take care of the tire."

"Afraid I can't let you do that, Kendra." Cameron planted his hands on his hips, emphasizing the power in his arms and the gun on his hip. "This is my jurisdiction, ma'am, and I believe there's an ordinance that states I must aid stranded motorists in my town or suffer serious consequences."

Her left eyebrow shot up. "You're kidding."

"Would I do that?" Absolutely. There wasn't any

such ordinance, but he wasn't about to tell her that? "If I don't make sure your vehicle's safe to drive in this town, I'd be breaking my own laws."

"What laws?"

"The ones that say I'd have to write myself a ticket."

"Go ahead. I don't mind."

"*I* would." He had her, he knew it by the twinkle in her pretty eyes. "Might even have to throw myself in jail and that's not how I want to spend my day."

"So, why would I care? I'm perfectly capable of changing the tire."

"Yeah, but I have a flawless record. Not a single infraction to date. You wouldn't want my reputation besmirched, would you?"

"Sure I would."

Humor tugged at the corners of her soft, lush mouth. Cam felt some pride about that. Kendra McKaslin might look cool and unapproachable, but she seemed like a real nice lady.

He'd been trying to approach her for the last few months, but he had a lot of questions about horses. He didn't know where to start. He didn't want to look like a dummy. After all, a man had his pride.

But Kendra didn't strike him as someone who'd made anyone feel dumb. She seemed as sweet as spring, with her long blond hair shimmering down her back like liquid gold in the sunlight. She'd grown up in one of the wealthier families in their humble valley, but was she snooty?

No. Down to earth, filled with common sense, Kendra was country-girl goodness soul-deep. He could *feel* it. He'd watched her kindness to her horses every time she'd ridden one of them into town on an errand to the store or to visit her family's coffee shop.

She appeared to be real good with the animals. Everyone said she was the best in the area when it came to horsemanship. But he hadn't gotten up his courage to talk to her.

Now was his chance. "I know you're an independent kind of woman. You're more than capable of changing that tire on your own."

"So why are you still standing here?" The hint of her smile grew into a real one.

"I've got an election coming up. What would folks think if they see you stranded here in obvious need of help—"

"Stranded? I don't think so!"

"Still, they'll watch me drive off and leave you behind and draw their own conclusions. All folks will see is that their elected official abandoned a woman stuck along the side of the road, slacking off on his duties."

"Like anyone would think you were a slacker."

"I can't risk it. Folks might vote for my opponent come September. I'd lose my job. Won't be able to pay my bills. You don't want to be responsible for that, do you?"

"Sure." There were more sparkles in her pretty blue eyes.

She had a quiet kind of beauty, one that wasn't only skin-deep.

His chest gave a strange hitch in the vicinity of his heart as he opened the truck's door for her. That was odd, considering how he hadn't felt much beside grief since Deb's death. "Your sister's sign is still on in the window. Why don't you go in, say hello and get something cool to drink? Give me twenty minutes and I'll have this taken care of."

"That's not right. It's my trailer."

"Yeah, well, it's a slow day. I don't see a lot of wild speeders or crime sprees on Thursday afternoons. It's okay to let me do this, Kendra."

He could see the argument coming. He'd learned to read people during his fifteen years wearing a badge. He saw a woman used to doing things herself. "If it bothers your conscience, then you can bring a batch of cookies or something by the station. My deputy has a sweet tooth you wouldn't believe."

She swept down from the seat with an easy grace that she didn't seem aware of.

He was. It sure threw him for a loop.

Today she looked summery and girl-next-door fresh in a white tank top, a pair of jean shorts and slip-on tennis shoes. Her blond hair, streaked by time in the sun, was tied back in a long ponytail. She slipped her sunglasses from the top of her head onto her nose and circled around the rig to look at the damage.

"I think my spare went flat." She said it wearily,

more to herself than to him. Probably expecting some kind of reprimand.

Why would he do that? Didn't a woman who worked hard to make her own living deserve a break? He sure thought so. "Zach's at his garage. I'll take the tire over for him to patch."

"He's my brother-in-law, and I can do it."

"Toll House, no walnuts. I have a soft spot for butterscotch chips.

He left her standing there, watching him with a slack jaw as he yanked the jack from his cruiser's trunk. "I'm helping you, no matter what. Just accept it."

"I should help you."

"Why? It would make me look bad. I've got my public image to think about. Voters care about that kind of thing."

He didn't care about his image, he worked hard to do the right thing and he was proud of his record. He had time, and in helping her maybe he'd find a way to approach her. Ask her professional opinion. "I'm not taking no for an answer. Your only option is to let me do my job."

She studied him and the jack he was carrying and the nearly flat tire. "Fine. Thank you. The horses—"

"Will be fine. I've done this before."

"Okay."

She didn't sound happy, but Cameron bet that she'd let him do it. He wasn't about to budge, he'd been waiting for this chance forever, that's what it felt like.

If he had a choice, then he'd want her to stay and watch so they could talk while he worked.

He knew her well enough to know she wouldn't hang around. She kept her distance from men, not just him, and with good reason.

He felt her sadness every time he was around her. Now maybe he was imagining it, because he'd been there to arrest Jerrod Melcher, and he saw how bad she'd been hurt. That was likely to make any woman wary about men for a long time.

It was understandable.

As he watched her cross the road, jaywalking, heading straight to her family's coffee shop, a streak of pain jabbed through his heart. A widower was used to feeling a certain amount of pain down deep, but this was something different. Something that felt a lot like longing.

One thing was for sure. When Kendra looked at him, she didn't feel any positive emotion. Not a chance. When she looked at him she remembered that night. He could feel that, too.

Perhaps he should just leave her alone. Ask Sally at the Long Horn Stables for help instead.

Frustrated, he got to work.

It was *her* trailer, she ought to be dealing with it. But that stubborn sheriff had refused to leave, so what was she going to do? Stand there and make small talk? She didn't need his help and she was getting it anyway. It ate at her as the bell over the coffee shop's door jangled.

The welcome breeze from the air-conditioning skimmed over her, but it didn't cool her anger. Men were bossy, every one of them. Who did the sheriff think he was that he could just do what he wanted to her trailer?

Face it, you appreciate that he's helping.

Sure, but it still bugged her. She was hot, exhausted, and dealing with a flat tire in over hundred-degree weather would have put her over the edge. Well, at least close to it.

Because of Cameron, she was able to rest for a few minutes instead of dealing with one more disaster in a doom-filled day. She didn't want to be grateful to him. But she was.

See why it was a good idea to stay far away from men? Even the nice ones?

"Kendra? You look too hot, are you all right?" Gramma sat at the far end of the otherwise empty room, behind one of the cloth-covered tables. Ignoring her spread of papers and her open laptop, she examined Kendra over the lines in her bifocals. "Something *is* wrong. Why are you back so soon?"

"I'm fine and it's past closing time." Kendra flicked off the neon sign and turned the Open sign in the window to Closed. "How long have you been in here slaving over the bookkeeping?"

"Goodness, let me see." She checked her gold wristwatch. "For much longer than I thought!"

"You lose track of time when you're doing the books. I do the same thing."

"I suppose so!" Gramma took off her glasses and wiped them on the corner hem of her stylish summer blouse. "I've lost two dollars and seventy cents I can't find anywhere. I'd just finish the deposit and say, forget it. But it'll be all I think about when I get home. Come, dear, sit down. You look as though you've got too much sun."

"No need to fuss, I'm fine. I'm going to raid the kitchen and pray there are some leftovers in the fridge. I'm too beat to cook when I get home."

"I knew it. You work too hard, sweetie. You can't work every minute of every day."

"I take a few minutes off now and then."

"Don't sass me, young lady. You've been skipping meals."

"Not intentionally."

Kendra ducked into the kitchen to avoid the lecture. She knew what was coming when Gramma got started. She loved her grandmother within an inch of her life, but how Gramma fussed! Kendra yanked open the industrial refrigerator and studied the contents. Jackpot!

Gramma's sandals tapped on the floor, announcing her approach to the kitchen.

"I can do it myself." Kendra pulled a bowl of chicken salad from the top shelf. "Do you want me to make you a sandwich, too?"

"Me? You're the one needing to eat. Give me that. Where's the mayonnaise?"

"I said I'd do it and I meant it." Kendra wrapped her grandmother into a hug and breathed in the honeysuckle sweetness of her perfume. "You've had a long day, and you don't need to make it longer by doing one single thing for me. You work too much."

"I've got good help. The girls I've hired this summer have been a real blessing. There's the macaroni salad you like in the bottom shelf. No, let me get it."

Kendra snatched the big stainless-steel bowl from the shelf. "Out. Go back to your table. Shoo!"

"Nice try, but I wrote the book on bossy." Gramma dug through the pantry and came up with a wrapped loaf of homemade bread. "We'll both fix us something to eat while you tell me about your new horses."

"You're a tricky woman, Gramma."

"Thanks, dear, I try. Hand me the serrated knife."

Kendra did as she was asked and found two plates while she was digging through the dishwasher. "I won the bid for the prettiest mustangs I've gotten yet. One is as wild and mean as a bull, but the others have potential."

"You bought a mean horse?" Gramma's disapproval wreathed her soft, lovely face, as she cut thick slices of wheat-nut bread. "Is that safe?"

"He's a stallion."

"I don't like the sound of that! Not at all. Boarding and training horses is one thing. But a stallion? How will you handle him? And he's wild, to boot!"

"I have a little tiny eensy-beensy bit of experience with horses, remember?" Kendra twisted open the jar of mayo. "I've been riding since before I could walk."

"I didn't approve of that, either, the way your father would put you and your sisters on the backs of horses when you were nothing but toddlers!" Gramma's eyes twinkled, though. "He must be a good-looking horse, if you bought him."

"He's a beauty. Bright chestnut coat. Perfect white socks. A long black mane and tail. And his lines... he's got some Arabian in him." Kendra sighed. "Of course, he gives new meaning to the word *wild.* I'm sure I can tame him, so don't start worrying. I haven't been killed by a horse yet."

"Heavens, I should hope not! You *do* have a way with them. I don't doubt that." Gramma bit her lip as she layered meat mixture and cheese on a slice of bread. As if she were thinking better of saying anything more.

Kendra whipped the knife from her grandmother's hand. "You go sit down. I'll finish this up and bring you a cup of iced tea to the table. Go. Away with you."

"You're getting just as bossy as me. I like that." Planting a kiss on Kendra's cheek, she left the kitchen without further complaint.

That wasn't like Gramma at all, but Kendra was too exhausted to dwell on it. She put away the sandwich makings, grabbed two bottles of iced tea from the case, shouldered through the swinging doors and into the silent shop.

With the wide bank of windows along the end wall, she had a perfect view of Cameron. He was rolling the tire across the street, apparently whistling as he went, looking like a hero in his navy-blue uniform.

"That Durango boy's helpin' you out, I see," Gramma commented as she tapped keys on her computer. "Funny that you'd let a man do something like that for you."

"Don't go reading something into it that's not there."

"Is something there?"

How many times had they discussed this? "I'm not going to get married, you know. Ever. So don't start getting your hopes up. The truth is, I'm so tired I can barely pick up my feet and Cameron offered to help me. He helps with this kind of thing all the time."

"Which kind of thing would that be? A tire low on air? Or helping a very pretty eligible woman?" Gramma's eyes twinkled as if she knew something Kendra didn't.

"If you're going to torture me about this, I'm taking my food and I'm leaving." Kendra said it lightly, but she meant it.

The impenetrable titanium walls around her heart were sealed shut. They were going to stay locked tight. "I'm not interested in Cameron."

"Then why, sweetie, is he fixing that tire for you?"

"Because he's a sheriff and I had a long day in the hot sun and no lunch."

She took a big bite of her sandwich to prove it.

"Fine. All right. I believe you." She held up her hands helplessly. "You can't blame a poor grandmother for hoping."

"Oh, yes I can!"

"Only three of my granddaughters are married and have given me perfect grandchildren. There's no crime in wanting more. Marge's youngest girl married just last year and had a new baby boy last week. That makes for four grandchildren for her. I've got to keep up."

Kendra rolled her eyes, her mouth too full to speak. What was the point? As if Gramma listened anyway. She had her definite opinions and nothing short of laser fire was going to change her mind.

"Cameron is certainly a good man, isn't he? He's so nice and courteous. Everyone raves on about what a fine sheriff he's been."

"Yes, I'm sure he'll be reelected. Now, can we change the subject?"

"Look how handsome he is in his uniform. I have a weakness for men in uniforms myself. The first time I saw your grandfather in his dress blues…it does make a girl feel safe, doesn't it?"

"Stop." Laughter escaped anyway. How could she be mad at her grandmother who so obviously loved the idea of marriage and happily-ever-afters?

But it wasn't for everyone. It even said so in the

Bible. God chose different paths for everyone and some women were meant to be married and mothers.

She wasn't. It hurt, but there wasn't anything she could do to change the direction her life had taken.

It wasn't as if she were alone.

Look at the blessings the good Lord had placed in her life. Her grandmother, her parents, her sisters, her friends and her horses. How many people actually got to do what they loved for a living? She'd always wanted her own riding stable, and that's what she had. She wasn't going to complain about her life. Not now. Not ever.

"Oh, where are the books off? This is the most aggravating thing on earth. Who invented bookkeeping, anyway? Whoever he is, he's a very bad man." Gramma's frustration was good-natured as she held up her hand and gave the computer a death-ray glare. "I should just quit, but it'll keep bothering me if I do."

"You're just tired. Let me take a peek." Kendra pulled the ledger so it faced her. "It's probably just a transposition."

"You are simply a wonder, my dear. Thank you."

As she ate, Kendra squinted at the numbers and tried to make her eyes focus. Minutes ticked by as she studied the long row of numbers and paired them against the deposit slip. It had to be a coincidence that she'd chosen a seat that faced the windows, right? She wouldn't pick this spot on purpose because she had a perfect view of Cameron Durango kneeling in the hot sun, working alongside Zach, her brother-in-law, who must have come over to help.

He may be handsome and kind and dependable, sure, but the steel doors around her heart stayed locked.

"Where are the checks?" Kendra tore her gaze from the window and noticed her grandmother's eyes were sparkling, as if she'd noticed where Kendra's gaze kept straying. "Oh, I get it. You think I'm interested in the sheriff."

"Oh, no. Of course not." She was the perfect face of innocent grandmotherly denial. "I was just thinking what a blessing it is that God sends us what we need when we need it most."

"And that cryptic comment means…"

"Oh, nothing about Cameron coming to help you when you needed it, of course. Heavens, no! I was referring to you walking through the door when I was ready to give up in frustration. The checks are here, in the bank bag."

Kendra waited while her grandmother slid the small dark bag across the table. Liar. Whether Gramma admitted it or not, *she* wasn't fooled one bit.

Why argue about it? There was no point. Her grandmother would come to understand in time and to accept Kendra's choices in life.

Cameron Durango, no matter how striking and protective and capable he looked in his uniform, would never be one of her choices.

Why did that make her sad? She decided her barricades were weakening, probably because she was still so tired and hungry.

See? A girl needed to keep up her strength so she wasn't susceptible to random, pointless emotions. It *was* pointless to feel sad about what could never be made right.

She bit into the second half of her sandwich and went to work comparing the thick pile of checks against the deposit slip.

Chapter Two

"Here's your problem, Gramma. It's right here. You've transposed a check amount on the deposit slip." Kendra grabbed the nearby pen and made the corrections. "There. That should do it."

"Wonderful! My dear, what would I have done without you?"

"You'd have found it without my help. I—"

The bell above the door jingled.

Cameron. She didn't need to turn around to know it was him. She *felt* his presence as surely as the current of August heat radiating through the opened door.

Why was she so aware of this man she hardly knew, as if he'd reached out and laid his hand on her arm? It was odd. She'd never felt this before with him or with anyone.

The door clicked shut, and he stood in the direct blast of the air-conditioning vent. Hat off, eyes closed, his head tilted back in appreciation. He seemed to be enjoying the icy draft as it ruffled his short, dark hair.

"That sure cooled me down." He clutched his hat in his big, capable hands. There was a streak of grease across the backs of his broad knuckles. "Good afternoon, Helen."

"Sheriff." Gramma's pleasure warmed her voice. "It's good to see you. Come in and cool down. Kendra will get you something to drink."

"Oh, I will?"

Leave it to her grandmother to try to matchmake. As if it would do any good. And poor Cameron. He was struggling to be elected, and he had to be *desperate* if he wanted to change her tire in this heat. He shouldn't have to keel over from heat stroke because of it.

The chair groaned in the joints as she stood, although it could have been her knees, but she didn't want to think about the creaks in her joints since she'd turned thirty. Her tennies squeaked on the clean floor as she put as much distance between her and Cameron as she could.

"Iced tea or soda?"

"One of those flavored teas would do just fine." Cameron followed her, as if he wasn't about to let her escape until he had her vote. Surely that's what this was all about.

She wasn't so sure when she turned around, with the cool metal handle in hand, and didn't notice the icy draft from the refrigeration unit. He was behind her, and this time she didn't tremble. She fizzed, like those carbonated bubbles in a glass of cola. She felt bubbly down deep in her soul.

"Lemon-flavored, if you've got it." His voice came warm, deep and as inviting as ever.

The bubbles inside her fizzed upward and she felt lighter than air. As if her soul turned upside down and wasn't sad anymore. How wrong was that? Get a grip, girl.

She handed him the squat bottle. "Anything else?"

"This is all I need." He didn't move away as he covered the mouth of the bottle with his wide palm and twisted the cap. "Zach lent a hand, too, so we did double-time getting it done. You're all set."

"Thanks, Sheriff."

"Cameron. I've loosened your lug nuts, I think we ought to be on a first-name basis."

"Aren't you funny?"

"I try to be. I get that way when I'm sugar-deprived."

"I can take a hint. You want more of a reward for a job well done? My vote isn't enough."

"I could use a snack."

Was it her imagination, or was he trying to be charming? "Does the town council know what you're up to?"

"Why? I'm doing nothing wrong. Every cop has the civil right to doughnuts. Or those amazing chocolate cookies your grandmother makes if you happen to have any lying around taking up too much space on your shelves.''

He was definitely trying to be nice. It was hard to shoot down a man complimenting Gramma's baking. Maybe that was one way to win elections. What did she know about politics?

''It's your lucky day.'' Kendra spied two chocolate cookies left over from the day's sales, looking lonely on the pastry shelf below the hand-off counter. ''Could you do us a favor and take them off our hands?''

''I reckon I could try. Helping the lovely ladies of this town is my beholden duty.''

He sure *must* want to be reelected, since he was trying so hard. As if he had any real competition anyway. From what everyone said, he'd been one of the best sheriffs the town had ever had. She grabbed the two cookies with a slice of waxed paper and handed them over.

He had a nice smile. Not flashy or too wide, but honest and easy. Sincere. ''My stomach thanks you. Helen, every time I see you zipping around in that little red convertible of yours, I think I've got to get me one of those.''

''Nah, you're too stodgy, young man.'' Gramma teased as she zipped up the bank's deposit bag. ''You're better off in that sensible SUV you drive.''

''You're making me sound middle-aged, Helen. I don't appreciate that.''

''It's not my fault you're stuffy.'' Laughing, Gramma

slipped the laptop into her shoulder bag and, clutching the deposit, she headed for the door. Much faster than usual.

"Gramma, where are you off to in such a hurry?"

"The bank."

"It's already closed."

As if she'd temporarily gone deaf, Gramma didn't answer, just smiled sweetly as she backed through the doorway. "You keep up the good work, young man. It's reassuring to see a man who knows responsibility."

Her grandmother tossed Kendra a knowing wink before snapping the door shut with a final jangle of the bell. That matchmaker!

"What was that about?" Cameron looked puzzled, which proved he couldn't be the best detective.

"It wasn't obvious? My other sisters are married off and providing her with grandchildren, so she's trying to find me a husband, I guess. Sorry about that." Kendra rolled her eyes as she grabbed her half-full bottle from the table.

"Hey, I understand. My grandmother is the same way. She asked me for years every time I saw her, which was every Sunday for church, why I couldn't find a nice girl and settle down." He ambled toward the door, talking conversationally.

The good-natured banter lifted a weight from her shoulders. Cameron was no threat. He was simply making conversation. He'd treated Gramma the same exact way.

More at ease, she followed him and dug in her shorts pocket for her keys. "So, how did you handle your grandmother?"

"I informed her that if I could find a nice girl, then I would marry her. The problem is finding a woman who's interested in *me*."

"Sure, I can see why that's a problem." Dependable man, handsome and fit and went out of his way to help others. She locked up and tested the lock— sometimes it was tricky.

"Once she saw it from a prospective bride's viewpoint, she stopped bothering me. She wouldn't want to inflict any nice girl with a husband like me."

"There's more to life than having a ring on your hand, that's for sure."

Was it a lie if you wanted to mean what you said, even if it wasn't the truth? Kendra wondered as she loped down the steps and crossed the street.

"Sure," he agreed, keeping stride with her.

Was it marriage she was against, or the fear of trusting a man that much?

They'd reached his cruiser. "You should be safe to drive home."

"Thanks again, Cameron. You have a good evening." She strode around the back of the trailer, jingling her keys in the palm of her hand as she went, blond hair blowing in a long silken ponytail behind her.

Cameron bit into a cookie as he waited by his cruiser to make sure she got on her way all right.

Chocolate broke apart in his mouth, as rich as cake and made richer with sweet chunks of milk chocolate.

It *almost* soothed away his disappointment as Kendra's truck engine rolled over with an easy hum. Taillights winked on and the right blinkers flashed. She eased out into the empty street leaving only tire marks and a hint of dust in the air.

That didn't bode too well, man. She was sure quick to get rid of him. Not that he'd come across as an intelligent future customer. No, he'd yakked on about his re-election when what he should have done was ask her about the boarding fees at her stable.

Seeking refuge inside the car, he started the engine and flicked the air-conditioning on high. Not even the second chocolate cookie made him feel better.

Maybe some things weren't meant to be. And if they were, then wouldn't the Lord present him with another chance?

He was upset, and it wasn't only about the questions he *didn't* ask Kendra. He'd fibbed when she'd asked how he'd handled his grandmother's desire for him to marry. His nana was a fine woman, a real lady, and she worried about him being alone.

The truth was, he'd lost his heart when he buried his wife. He'd lived in darkness ever since her passing. His grieving was done, but the loneliness remained.

He'd loved being married. If he could find a woman that filled him up like sunlight, that made him alive again, well, wouldn't that be something? Did true love happen twice in a lifetime?

He'd leave that answer up to the Lord. In the meantime, his workday was done. There was nothing else to do but go home. He would face the lonely house and the silent kitchen as he did every night and make a tuna-fish sandwich for supper while he listened to the world news.

Alone.

Alone. *Finally.* Kendra collapsed on her secondhand couch and let the window unit pummel her with blessed, cold air. Her fat tabby cat meowed a weak protest from the top of the cushion, but his demand for more treats was the last one in a long list.

She'd done everything. The new horses were in the paddock, the stalls in the stables were cleaned, the horses fed and watered, the trailer hosed out. She'd returned messages, paid a few bills and checked on a pregnant mare.

The cat's meow was louder.

"Pounce, can you wait two minutes? Just two? I don't think I can move."

Meow.

"The treats are on the other end table. I can't reach them from here."

Apparently tired of her excuses, the twenty-pound orange tabby leaped off the top of the cushion and onto Kendra's stomach.

"Okay, I'll get the treats." Laughing, she rubbed

the cat's head, as he purred. The shrill ring of the phone had her reaching for the cordless handset tossed in the mess on the coffee table. "This had better be good."

"Ooh, it is!" It was her littlest sister Michelle, trembling with excitement. Not that Michelle was all that little now that she was grown-up and married. "We're all on our way to the hospital. Karen was admitted about thirty minutes ago."

"She's having the baby?" Excitement must have reenergized her, because Kendra found the will to stand up, carrying Pounce as she crossed the room. "Did you need a ride or is your hubby there?"

"Brody's locking up right now… Oops, I gotta go. He's dragging me to the front door." Michelle was laughing. "See you at the hospital!"

Another niece or nephew to welcome into their family! Kendra tossed the phone onto the cushions to worry about later. She was going to be an aunt— again. She had to hurry. She had to drive. She needed caffeine. Good thing she'd made a pitcher of sun tea yesterday.

A swift brush along her ankles reminded her of her primary mission. The cat led the way to the treat bag and his demanding meow left no doubt. He was annoyed with her.

"I know, that phone was more important than you. I'm sorry, buddy." She gave him an extra treat, rubbed his head while he purred gratefully and made the long journey of about seven steps into the small galley kitchen.

Okay, so she hadn't done *all* her chores today. Bypassing the counter of dirty dishes, she rummaged through the back of the cupboard until she found a clean cup, dumped some sugar in for good measure and went in search of her keys.

Where were they? The cat was no help, as he was settling on his cushion in front of the air conditioner and couldn't be bothered with lowly human dilemmas.

"Found 'em!" On the floor beneath her tennies. "Bye, Pounce!"

The cat managed a disdainful frown, which Kendra took to mean he'd miss her.

Twilight was creeping into the long shadows as she started her truck, but that didn't provide any relief from the heat. No. At least she wasn't towing a trailer, so she punched up the air-conditioning. The sinking sun blazed bright orange and magenta in her rear and side-view mirrors, tailing her as she headed to Bozeman.

The sun had set in a lavender hush by the time she pulled into the hospital parking lot, found an available space as close to the front doors as she could manage and climbed out into the coming darkness.

"Kendra, is that you?" A man's voice rumbled behind her.

Her keys tumbled through her fingers and crashed to the pavement at her feet. She recognized his deep, warm baritone instantly. Smooth move, Kendra. "Cameron. What are you doing here?"

"Startling you. Here, let me." He knelt and retrieved her keys.

It was gentlemanly of him. If he hadn't spoken first, she might not have realized it was him right off. She was used to seeing him in his navy-blue uniform. Tonight he wore a simple T-shirt and jeans, belted at his lean hips, and scuffed boots.

He straightened to his full six feet and held her key ring on the wide palm of his hand. "I've come to your rescue again."

"I guess. If you hadn't come along when you did, I'd have been in a real dilemma, being unable to pick up my own keys."

"See? Glad I could be of service."

"And just what are you doing here anyway? Following me?"

"You'd have noticed in your rearview if I had. Nope, my pager went off halfway through my supper. Big wreck on the highway."

She'd taken the back road to Bozeman, not the highway. "Was anyone hurt?"

"A tire blew out, and the driver was injured. It was the father of a family on their summer vacation."

"Will he be all right?"

"Broke his leg. He'll be spending the night in the hospital, so I told him I'd make sure his wife and kids get settled into a hotel room. During tourist season, you don't know the strings I had to pull for that one."

"That was decent of you."

"Yeah? Well, I try not to be such a bad guy, considering I wear a badge and give people tickets."

"I've heard you cops have unfair quotas to fill."

"Pressure of being a cop." His smile broke wide, showing a row of straight even white teeth and a hint of a dimple. "Why do I have the pleasure of running into you on this fine evening?"

"I'm about to become an aunt again."

"Congratulations." He fell in step beside her. "That's hard work, becoming an aunt."

"Yeah, I have it much harder than Karen. I have to shop in the gift store. I have to sit and wait in those uncomfortable chairs."

"There must be an unspoken but ironclad law in hospital administration that states they can only allocate funds for the most uncomfortable chairs on the planet. They would *have* to buy them on purpose. There's no way they could find those chairs by chance."

"There's an administrator somewhere in this building who has better job security because of it."

The lobby was quiet this time of evening. To Kendra's surprise Cameron stayed by her side as they wound their way to the elevators. He punched the Up button.

An uncomfortable silence stretched between them while they both watched the lit numbers move up and not down in their direction.

What did she say now? She was horrible at making small talk.

A janitor rolled his cart into sight and ambled to the far corner of the lobby. He began washing windows.

Cameron broke the silence. "Did you get your horses all tucked in for the night?"

"Yep."

"That had to be tough. They can't be used to being cooped up in a trailer."

"No, but I've worked with a lot of horses over the years. I sweet-talked them."

Cam could see it in his mind as the doors parted and he followed Kendra inside the elevator. Her gentle words and gentle hands, her quiet ways that told those frightened animals only good things were going to happen to them while they were in her care.

See? He'd asked the Lord for another chance and this was it. He had Kendra alone. Trapped, as it were, in the elevator with him. Folks probably asked her advice all the time.

So just do it. He punched the floor button and leaned against the wall. The car zipped upward, reminding him he had only so much time. "Say, how much does it cost if someone wanted to board a horse at your place?"

Her pretty eyes widened. Had he surprised her that much? She unzipped her good-size purse and started digging through the contents. "It depends. I think I have a price list in here. There are different rates depending on the level of care you want and size stall, feeding plans, training and exercising, that kind of thing.''

Her hair was unbound, and it was full of light, falling to cover her face as she rummaged past a worn leather wallet and a glasses case. He took his time looking his fill, while she was busy and wouldn't notice him gawking at her.

She was prettiest this close, he decided. He could see the scatter of light freckles across her nose and cheeks, probably brought out by the summer sun, on skin golden brown and as smooth as satin.

''Here it is.''

He jerked his gaze to the floor at her scuffed white sneakers, as if he hadn't been looking anywhere else.

The rattle of paper drew his attention. He straightened up, all business. It was hard holding back his emotions, but he was a disciplined man with a plan. He admired the cut of her hands, slender and suntanned, callused from her work, with neat short nails painted a shimmering pink.

It dawned on him that she was waiting for him to take the neat brochure. ''Uh, thanks.''

''I didn't know you had a horse.''

He opened the trifolded lavender paper and stared at numbers that made no sense. His brain couldn't seem to work right. He couldn't believe what he was about to do. Don't back out now, man.

He cleared the nerves from his throat before he spoke. ''I don't. Yet.''

Now there was a dazzling show of his mastery of the language.

She didn't seem to notice. If she did, then she managed to keep her pity for his sorry conversational skills to a minimum. Her voice was as warm as her smile. "You can ask me if you have any questions."

"Or I could just pull you over the next time you drive through town."

"Aren't you funny? Abusing your power as an authority figure." She teased him in return—she couldn't help it—as the doors opened to the maternity wing. "Have a good night, Cameron."

"You, too. Congratulations on becoming an aunt again."

He was gone; the doors slid shut before she could answer, leaving her alone. The chug and chink of the elevators echoed in the quiet. She turned around, eyes down because she knew what was ahead of her.

The viewing window of the nursery where newborns slept tucked tight in their blankets and beds, their dear button faces either relaxed in slumber or screwed up in misery as they cried. A nurse was lifting one tiny unhappy baby into her arms as Kendra passed by.

Don't look. Keep moving.

Her feet refused to work, leaving her trapped in front of the window. It hurt to look. It hurt not to look. She admired the tiny babies, their perfectly formed miniature hands, their sweet faces, and envied their lucky parents.

How was it possible to feel happy *and* sad at the same moment? Happy for the precious new babies and sad because she would never have one of her own.

How could she? She wasn't ever going to date. Never going to marry. Never trust a man that much.

There would be no babies for her.

The grief struck her as it always did like a boxer's blow to her sternum. It was her choice, her decision. She couldn't complain. She wouldn't feel sorry for herself, but when would this consuming longing end?

She turned away before the ache within her could crescendo. Before regret and loss could swallow her whole.

Her sisters were waiting beyond those imposing double doors. Why were her feet dragging? What was holding her back?

It was hard to face how different her life was, from what she'd always thought it would be. That's what. She'd wanted to be a wife and a mother. A horse-woman, yes, but, oh, to be truly and deeply loved by a good man. To have her own children to love and nurture. What could be more important than that?

Don't think about what might have been. She closed her eyes, hoped the Lord would help her find the strength to face her family behind those doors without feeling sorrow over the what-ifs in her life. As hard as it was to see what she might have had, she was truly happy for her sisters and their families. To the depth of her soul.

It wasn't as if she was alone. She was an aunt; she

would always have children in her life. She *would* count the wonderful blessings the Lord had given her.

Not dwell on the ones missing.

She squared her shoulders, forced every piece of grief from her heart. She was ready. Behind that door were her sisters and their husbands and their children. Her warm extended family she loved with all her being.

She refused to feel sad, not tonight. Not when there was so much to celebrate. So much to be grateful for.

Cameron couldn't stop thinking about the brochure he'd folded and tucked into his shirt pocket. His mind was half on it all during the time he made sure Mr. Anderson had what he needed for the night. Those prices were reasonable. Better than what he'd expected.

I can do this. Excitement zoomed through him as he gave Anderson the number of the hotel his family was staying at. Optimism gave him extra zing as he punched the elevator call button and waited for an empty car in the quiet hush of the corridor.

Money had been tight for a long time, what with Debra's medical costs and funeral expenses, and selling their house, he'd had to come up with the cash to pay for the closing. He'd worried that buying a horse might be a much more expensive proposition than he could afford, now that his finances were evening out.

The elevator doors opened, the empty car waiting to take him downstairs. He hit the Lobby button and pulled out the brochure as the elevator descended, clicking off the floors.

It had been a long, hard road taking care of Deb, not as hard as the road she walked with her illness. It nearly killed him having to say goodbye to her. Faith saw him through that tough time and after. He'd only been existing, not living. How did a man live with only half of a heart?

Memories tugged him back in time, when he and Deb were newlyweds. Their budget was tight. It had to be. She was finishing up her legal-assistant course at the technical college while he was hoofing it through the academy. Part-time jobs kept them in a small one-bedroom apartment not far from the campus in Bozeman. They had to work to make ends meet, but Deb had made it fun. She was so easy to laugh with. They laughed all the time.

He missed that. He missed the dreams they would talk about over doing the dishes by hand in the cramped kitchen. Deb wanted a sprawling house just out of town, so she could see trees instead of neighbors.

He'd wanted enough land to graze a horse or two on. She'd liked that idea, and wove more dreams of how it would be when times were better, riding their horses in their fields. What a great life they were going to have. Together.

Grief weighed down his soul.

The elevator inched to a halt and the doors whispered open. The outside world beyond the long wall of lobby windows was dark, and he hated the thought of going out in it.

She'd been gone four years, and the pain of heading home to an empty house still ate at him.

Is that going to change anytime soon, Lord?

Then he saw Kendra through a glass partition in the far wall. The overhead light haloed her golden hair and caressed her creamy complexion. She wore a simple T-shirt and her denim shorts, nothing pretty or fancy or extraordinary, and she looked so lovely.

He supposed it was loneliness that made him look. He missed a woman's presence in his life. The softness and gentleness, the little bottles all over the bathroom counter… He missed all of it.

It was a puzzle, because he'd seen plenty of women over the years. Not one of them made him feel as if the world had simply melted away until there was only her.

She didn't know he was watching as she leaned against the counter, turning to talk to her sister. She sparkled, laughing, tilting back her head to study the array of cheerful balloons floating just out of reach.

He couldn't say why that was, but as he strolled through the automatic doors and out into the parking lot, the night didn't seem as bleak or as lonely as it had been before.

Chapter Three

Squinting against the bold afternoon sun blinding her through the windshield, Kendra set the emergency brake. Okay, how was she going to do this? The cookies were in the back seat, all ready to go, but her sister was in the passenger seat beside her. Michelle was bound to notice what was going on.

If only she'd had more time! The day following Anna's birth had been jam-packed with errands and work and visits to the hospital. Mom and baby were coming home this evening, and there was a lot of work still to be done.

She'd been lucky to get the cookies baked. By the time she might get the chance to deliver them again all by herself, they would be beyond stale and as hard as bricks.

Please don't make a big deal over this, she silently begged Michelle, who was rummaging through her purse looking for her lipstick. Good, she was distracted. "You wait right here where it's cool. Don't move a muscle. I'll be just a second."

"Wait! Where are you going? I thought those cookies were for us." Michelle's hand, holding the found lipstick, rested on the small round bowl of her pregnant belly. "They're not for us?"

"Nope."

"I need cookies."

"Don't worry. I saved a small plate for you."

"But—"

Oh, no, here came the questions! Kendra slammed the door shut before Michelle could get out one more word. Not that she'd succeeded in keeping her mission secret. No, if anything, she was simply delaying an explanation.

Michelle was bound to notice what was going on, since she had a perfect view of the office's front door. She would be pelted with questions on her return as to why she was leaving cookies for the town's handsome and available sheriff.

Would Michelle believe the truth? Of course not! The truth was too boring. Her lovely sister would see romantic intent in a simple offering of thanks. Kendra would never hear the end of it.

This is what she got for doing the right thing. She heard the buzz of the window being lowered the instant she set foot on the sidewalk.

"Ooh, you've got a crush on that new deputy, don't you?" Michelle sparkled with complete delight. "Sis, you've got great taste. What's his name? Frank? I *knew* it. I knew the right man for you would come along if we prayed hard enough.''

See? *This* was exactly the type of thing she was trying to avoid. ''I don't have a crush on anyone.''

''Sure. I understand. You're doing your civic duty. Thanking the eligible bachelor who protects our town.''

''It's not like that.''

''Yep, sure, like I understand totally.'' Michelle feigned absolute empathy, but there was no mistaking that look on her face. ''I'm glad for you, Kendra. You deserve a fine man.''

Kendra opened her mouth to argue, but what would she say? Denial would only make it look like the truth. She loved Michelle for her kind words, but Michelle didn't know what had happened that night when everything changed.

There'd be no man for her. It was that simple. Kendra had been in love once and it had hurt worse than anything she'd ever known. She'd spent the last half-dozen years picking up the pieces of her life.

She would never give another man that much power over her. She would never trust a man that much. No matter what.

So Michelle could hope all she liked. She could think whatever she wanted. It would not change the facts.

The window buzzed upward, and Kendra could feel Michelle's elation. Now her entire family was going to hear about this. Yep, she definitely should have delivered the cookies later in the week, stale or not.

There was Cameron's cruiser, parked neatly against the curb, polished and spotless.

And why was she noticing it? Didn't she have enough on her mind with the thousand things she had to do next? She needed to clean Karen's house, catch her up on her laundry and do a thorough grocery shop so her pantry would be well stocked. Then she needed to figure out what was she going to cook tonight for dinner for her entire family. *That's* what she ought to be thinking about.

Not noticing that she had a perfect view of Cameron's desk through the generous front window. And her stomach should certainly *not* be doing little quakes, as if butterflies were trapped there.

Why was she feeling this way? There was nothing to be anxious about. She intended to say hello, leave the plate on his desk and walk back out. Nothing personal about it. There was nothing personal between them.

Thank the good Lord that's the way Cameron felt about her, too. It wasn't as if he thought, as Michelle did, that romance could be blossoming.

Before she could reach for the tarnished brass knob, the door swung open. Cameron, looking fine in his navy-blue uniform, took a step back.

His smile was dazzling. "Come in. I never turn away a woman bringing baked goods."

"It's bad form to turn away free food," a second man's voice commented from inside the office.

Kendra pushed her sunglasses off her nose and up over her forehead, and the shadows became a burly uniformed man sitting behind a desk in the corner, but she hardly noticed him. Cameron drew her attention as the surprise on his face turned to appreciation.

Appreciation for the cookies, no doubt. She handed him the covered paper plate. "I made a batch with butterscotch chip *and* my gramma's famous chocolate-chocolate chips."

"I don't think there are enough words to thank you." Cameron took the plate eagerly and ripped off the foil. "Frank, you've got to try these chocolate cookies. They sell them over at the coffee shop."

"Try them? Already have. I'm addicted to them."

"Your grandmother could charge ten bucks for a single cookie and folks would still buy two." Cameron snatched a cookie and took a bite.

"Ma'am, we sure do appreciate this." The deputy chose a chocolate cookie from the plate. "I'll just leave you two alone. I've got a report to file, uh, in the back room."

There was no back room. Cameron appreciated Frank's efforts, though, as the deputy disappeared into the storage closet, where they kept their coats and their spare office supplies.

That Frank was quick on the uptake. He saw right off that Kendra was the kind of woman a man wanted to be alone with instead of making small talk while other people watched.

"I hear your sister had her baby. A girl." Cameron held the plate out, offering her a cookie.

Kendra shook her head, declining the offer. "I have another beautiful niece. I'm pretty lucky, being an aunt. It's much better than being a parent, because I get all the snuggles and fun and I get to buy presents, but I don't have the sleepless nights and all the work that goes with it."

"Sounds like a good deal." Cameron wondered at the false brightness he saw on Kendra's face. A face that had small crinkles in the corners of her eyes, marks of character that he found attractive. Hers was not a face of sleek, artificial beauty, and a light within him flickered to life. "I'm glad to know Karen and her new baby are fine. Your other sister is expecting soon, isn't she?"

"Yes, in a few months. We have a lot of blessings to be thankful for in my family. And speaking of blessings, thank you again for help with the tire." Her sincerity shone soul-deep. "If these cookies aren't enough, I can bring by another batch sometime."

"This is more than enough." He'd never tasted a more delicious cookie. He'd never seen a more beautiful woman. There was so much to respect about Kendra, he didn't know where to begin, but if he made a list of all her attributes, it would be a long one.

She was certainly showing good manners in thanking him for helping her. After all, he'd told her he wouldn't be averse to receiving baked goods if she wanted to repay him, but she'd actually come. That said a lot about her.

He'd definitely go with her stables, if he decided he could afford a horse. That was a big question he needed an answer to if he was going to go any further with this notion of his.

"You have a good day, now." She was backing toward the door.

There was no time like the present while he had her here, even if she was halfway out the door. "Say, Kendra."

She hesitated, one hand on her black-rimmed sunglasses perched on the top of her head. She crooked one eyebrow in question.

He didn't wait for her to speak—or to escape. "I want to board my horse out at your place. Except there's one small catch."

"What's that?"

"I don't have a horse."

"Right. I remember you told me." A hint of a smile played along her soft mouth. "How are you going to board a horse you don't have at my place?"

"That's where you come in. I thought with your extensive horse knowledge combined with the fact that you don't want to lose my business to your competition—"

"Isn't that like extortion or something?"

"Sure, but I'm the law and I don't mind a little extortion if it gets me what I need."

Kendra couldn't help it. He made her laugh. Who knew the serious and capable town sheriff had a sense of humor? "I guess when the criminals are in charge, what's a poor business owner to do? How can I help?"

"I've looked in the classifieds and there seem to be plenty of horses for sale, but I don't know where to start. I don't know a thing about them. What's the difference between a quarter horse and a paint? Which is better? The prices seem to range from a hundred bucks to tens of thousands of dollars. I'm lost. I need help."

"I guess I'd better lend a hand, if I want to get your business."

"I knew you'd see things my way. I'd hate to have to tail you through town and ticket you under false pretenses until you cooperate."

"That would be a real bother."

So *that's* why he'd been acting friendlier than usual. He'd been too embarrassed to ask outright for help. Men were so funny. All ego and pride.

She wouldn't mind helping him at all, even if he didn't want to board at her stable. In this world, horse people had to help each other out.

"Why don't you come out to the stables this weekend sometime? Give me a call first, and I'll show you around the place and introduce you to different types of horses. We'll see what you like, and then you'll be able to figure out what you need. Then you can get an idea of cost."

"Sounds great. I'll do that."

"Good. You *do* know how to ride, don't you?"

"Uh, well, no. I've given it a lot of thought, and I've always wanted to ride."

"You're going to love it, don't worry. You're about to take the first step on a great adventure." She lit up, the way she'd been in the hospital's gift shop, all gentle radiance and happiness. "There is nothing like owning a horse. You'll see."

The first step on a great adventure, huh?

He closed the door and watched while she strolled toward her pickup parked neatly and legally along the curb. She was like sunshine and he felt that way whenever he looked at her. As if she brought light to the dark corners of his life. Warmth to the cold and lonely places.

Stunned, he didn't move a muscle. Just stood watching Kendra's green pickup pull out into the street, blinker flashing. What was that he just experienced? He didn't know, but he *thought* he liked it.

The hinges squealed as the closet door opened. "Is the coast clear?"

Cameron winced. He'd forgotten about Frank hiding out in the closet. "Sure, man. Come on out. She's gone."

"With your heart, by the looks of it." Frank stole another cookie. "She sure can bake. That's a decent trait in a woman. If you can trust one of them enough to marry."

"Marry her? Whoa. I helped her with a trailer tire."

"Whatever. I'm not gonna argue with you. But a woman like that, she's what? She's got to be over thirty. She's got that riding stable east of town, doesn't she?"

"I heard something like that."

"Careful, man. She's the kind that'll break your heart. Believe me. She's not looking for a husband. She's not the soft, gentle kind of female that needs a man."

"Oh, yes she is." Cameron knew something about Kendra that Frank didn't. What no one else in this town knew.

He well remembered the night when lightning had split the old willow tree in the town park. The fire department had been fighting to contain the blaze that was threatening the entire downtown. Power had been out all the way to Bozeman.

It was also the night he'd responded to a 911 call to a house near the railroad tracks in town.

He'd never forgotten that night. He suspected Kendra hadn't, either.

"It's about time you started dating again."

"Hi to you, too, Gramma." Kendra carefully laid her fragile, newborn niece down in her pretty well-appointed crib. "I'm not dating again."

"Then you're *thinking* about dating." Gramma eased to a stop at the railing.

"Not even thinking about it."

"Well, you *should* be. It's time, my dear. It's taken

you a long while getting over Jerrod. You really must have loved him.''

Kendra's throat ached at the sympathy in her grandmother's words. At the caring concern that had been there forever, it seemed. Her gramma had always been there to help her whenever she needed it. Except for that one time. That one horrifying time.

She shivered, forcing the truth away. "Can we please talk about something else?"

Unfortunately, her gramma refused to back down. I've gotten to know him when he comes in for early-morning coffee. He likes three straight shots to start his day.''

"I'm not interested in the new deputy. Michelle's exaggerating.'' How many times would she have to say that in the next hour?

"Then it's as I thought. The *sheriff.* Cameron Durango is as good as gold, if you ask my opinion. Sad it is, that he's a widower at his age. Not many know how hard he had it, taking care of his wife when she was ill. Cancer is a hard enemy.''

"I didn't know you knew Cameron so well.'' Kendra didn't know that about his wife.

She hadn't even known he'd been married. She could hardly keep up with her busy life. But it struck her hard, realizing that he was alone. He'd already lost everything that could matter, and he wasn't much older than she was.

"How long ago was that? I would have remembered the funeral.''

"His wife wasn't a member of our church."

That explained it. No wonder Cameron was looking for new activities to fill his leisure hours. A horse, what an excellent idea. Horses were more than pets, they were amazing, compassionate creatures. Most of her best friends had been horses.

Maybe Cameron could find the same kind of comfort she'd found.

"Michelle misunderstood. Cameron is interested in boarding a horse with me. That's all."

"Is he? I'm glad he's starting to live his life again. It takes time, getting over that kind of grief. I know you'll be good to him."

"As I am to all my clients." She hoped Gramma would get the hint.

"I know, dear, but a grandmother has to hope. Cameron would make a fine husband."

Kendra rolled her eyes. "You would have said the same about the deputy. Or anyone else, for that matter. You just want me to be married, like a good woman should be."

"That's right. While I believe a woman ought to wait for true love to come along, I know you would be happier with a husband of your own. With babies of your own."

Her own baby. Kendra ached in her soul, for that's how deep the yearning went—and how deep the wound.

Not that she could let anyone know. Not even Gramma. She swallowed hard, burying her pain.

"You're one to talk. You are a businesswoman. You said buying half of Karen's business was one of the best things you ever did."

"Yes, but I've been married. I've raised my family. There is a season for everything." Gramma brushed her hand over baby Anna's tuft of downy golden hair. "Hello, sweetheart. You are amazing, yes you are."

They stood together, side by side, gazing into the crib where the baby blinked up at them, drifting off to sleep.

"So soft." Love vibrated in her grandmother's voice. "There's nothing like a newborn life."

"Nothing so precious," Kendra agreed.

"There is one thing as precious. Love between a wife and her husband."

"You had to go and ruin the moment, didn't you?"

"I'm just getting my shots in while I can, dear. If you are lucky enough that true love finds you, my beautiful granddaughter, I hope you stop working at your business long enough to grab hold of what matters."

The wisdom in her grandmother's words left her shaky. Kendra didn't doubt the wisdom. True love *could* exist.

But to her? Never. It was a fact. "Are we done talking about this now?"

"I suppose." Gramma fell silent.

It was reassuring, watching over little Anna while she slept. She scrunched up her tiny rosebud mouth, looking even more adorable in her relaxed, peaceful slumber.

Faint noises from downstairs drifted along the hallway, Dad's low voice and Mom's gentle alto answering him. The *clank* of the oven door closing. The *clink* of silverware as someone was setting the table. The delicious aroma of the casserole Kendra had put in the oven. Mom must have taken it out to cool.

The sounds of family.

She did not take lightly this blessing the good Lord had given her. She had a big, loving extended family. She was thankful for them down to the depths of her soul.

There is one thing as precious. Love between a wife and her husband. Not for me, she told herself. Not ever.

Her life was enough. It *was*. She would not let her grandmother's kindly-meant words hurt.

"Isn't little Anna something?" Gramma sighed. "She looks like you did, you know. That little button nose. That round darling face. That's what your little girl will look like one day."

"Don't, Gramma." Gasping on pain, Kendra spun away, heading for the door.

"Honey, are you all right?"

"Sure."

It was only a half fib. She *intended* to be fine. Tucking away the raw hurt, she kept on going. Gramma needed time alone with her new great-granddaughter, and there was the supper to see to. Kendra was the self-appointed cook for the night, and she wasn't about to let someone else take over.

That's the reason she told herself for hurrying from the room. It wasn't because of the tears in her eyes. Of the sadness that haunted her through the days and into the nights of her solitary life.

Her cell buzzed in her back pocket. She wasn't in the mood for personal calls, but she withdrew the small handset and glanced at the screen. With her business, she was always on call, emergencies happened.

She saw with relief that it wasn't Colleen calling her from the riding stable. No, the name on the screen was Cameron Durango's.

She almost sent the call onto her voice mail, but she remembered what Gramma had told her. His wife had died. How difficult that had to be, to lose so much.

That's why he was calling. Why he'd helped her with the tire and took the time to talk to her in the hospital. He was looking to make a new life. To fill his empty time with new activities.

How could she *not* help him? She might never know the depth of what he'd lost when he buried his wife, but she understood heartache. She understood what a future with no love and no marriage looked like.

She answered the call. "Hi, Cameron. You must be pretty anxious to buy a horse."

"I guess I am." He had a good-hearted voice, kind and resonant. "You said to give you a jingle. That maybe you could find time for me to come over. Take a look around.''

"I'd be happy to help you out. I'll be working all morning tomorrow, but I should have a little free time after noon."

"How about one? Will that work?"

"One o'clock sounds fine. You know how to find me?"

"Wouldn't be much of a sheriff if I didn't."

"Good." The cool, polite tones had vanished from her alto voice, and she sounded friendly enough.

Cameron took that as an excellent sign. "I'll be there. I sure appreciate this, Kendra."

"No problem. Take care."

"You, too."

He hung up the phone, the silence of his small kitchen echoing around him. It had been a long time since he'd let hope into his heart.

How good it felt.

Chapter Four

Kendra sliced open the fifty-pound grain sack with her grandfather's Swiss Army knife, folded the blade away and tucked it safely into her jeans pocket. Sweat gathered along her forehead and trickled into her eyes.

She blinked against the sting, swiped her forehead with the back of her forearm and hefted the awkward sack onto her shoulder.

Was she thinking about her next riding class? Worrying about Willow's overdue foal? Hoping no riders took off on the out-of-bounds trail and ran into a hungry wolf or mountain lion?

No, of course not. What was she thinking about?

Cameron. Ever since she took an early lunch break and remembered he'd be showing up in a few hours.

Ever since she had checked her watch every few minutes, as if she was worried about missing him.

How crazy was that? Cameron was a grown man.

He was perfectly capable of finding her. It wasn't as if she were hiding in the woods. She was in plain sight from the paddocks. Since it was a busy Saturday with tons of people around, he'd have plenty of people to ask where to find her. That is, if he even showed up.

Stop worrying about him. She braced her feet, bent her knees and tipped the gunnysack forward. The ping and rush of falling grain sliding into the fifty-gallon drum echoed in the feed room, providing a welcome distraction. The sweet-scented dust sprinkled everywhere.

Was it one o'clock yet? Or a few minutes after? And what was with her that she kept wondering about him? It was what Gramma had said about him. It had touched her heart and taken root. *He's starting to live his life again. It takes time getting over that kind of grief.*

Sympathy welled up within her. He'd lost a wife to cancer, when they'd both been so young. It reminded her that tragedy happened to everyone, even the faithful. As much as she'd been hurt, other people had lost more. Been hurt worse.

She patted the last of the grain from the sack, grabbed the end corners and shook. Stragglers tumbled into the dusty heap and she coughed, breathing in the molasses-flavored dust.

She saw his polished black boots first at the edge of her vision as he hesitated just inside the doorway. His boots were unfamiliar to her, black and expensive but not tooled, and not a traditional riding boot.

That must be the reason she knew it was Cameron before she swept her gaze up the rock-solid length of his jeans, ignoring the holstered gun and pager at his belt, along the flat hard ridge of his abdomen and chest to the stony square of his jaw.

He wore a gray T-shirt, and reflective wraparound sunglasses hid his eyes. "You are one hard woman to find."

"I'm not hiding. Just working. There were plenty of people to ask where I was. Didn't anyone help you?"

"Didn't ask."

Ah, typical man. She should have known. Real men never ask for directions. No wonder she'd been worried about him finding her. She must have a sense about him, and how weird was that?

She tossed the empty gunnysack onto the pile in the corner.

"I'm glad to see you were brave enough to come."

"I'm no coward. Why, did you think I was?"

A coward? No one in their right mind would think that. Anyone who looked at him would think he was the bravest man ever. He emanated strength and heart. "A lot of folks call, but once they get out here and see how big horses are up close and personal, they miraculously change their minds."

"I may be a lot of things, but I'm no coward and I'm dumb enough to be proud of it."

"An honest man. I like that."

"Since I'm being honest, I guess I'd better admit

that I haven't seen any horses up close yet. My courage has yet to be tested."

"Why put it off? Come with me." She fastened the lid, locking it against field mice, and swung her Stetson from the hook on the wall. "I hope you came prepared."

"To ride?" The cords in his neck tensed. He stood rooted to the floor as she slid past him into the main breezeway.

"You look a little nervous, Officer."

"Me? Nervous? Nope." He squared his wide shoulders, like a soldier preparing for battle. "I face danger every day. Armed felons and criminals and gunfire. I'm not scared of a horse."

"I like your attitude," she replied over her shoulder as she led the way through the main stable.

"What attitude?"

"Confidence. You're going to need it."

His gait fell in stride with hers, easygoing but with a hint of tension. "Why do you say it like that? Like I've got something to fear and you're not gonna tell me what it is."

"Don't worry about it. There's nothing to fear. Really." She liked the crook of humor gathered in the corner of his mouth.

It wasn't fair to tease a little nervous, first-time rider, but Cameron looked so big and strong, like a man who couldn't ever be scared of anything, she couldn't resist. "You aren't afraid of hitting the ground hard, are you?"

"Who, me? No. Thanks to you, I'm so relaxed about this."

"I'm glad I could help." Biting her bottom lip to keep from laughing out loud—how long had it been since a man had made her laugh?—she stopped at the head of the aisle, where a long row of stalls marched through the bright sunlight from the skylights overhead to the far side of the stable.

A few horses came to look, peering over their gates, some nickering, some scenting in the direction of the stranger. Most of the stalls were empty. The scrape of a pitchfork in the distant corner accompanied the familiar scents of fresh alfalfa and straw.

"Sure is a nice operation you got here." Jamming his hands in his pockets, he took his time looking around. "Clean. Nice. Who did the construction, one of the outfits in town?"

"No. Me and my cousin Ben did. My dad helped out when he could."

She looked with pride at the building she'd put together with her own two hands. She'd had help, but she'd checked books out of the library and studied, and her neighbor, Mr. Brisbane, was a retired carpenter who liked giving her advice.

"*You* did this? A woman of many talents. I'm impressed."

"Not going to censure me?" Kendra relaxed as the corner of his hard, lined, masculine mouth cinched up in a grin. "I got a lot of that when I bought this place."

"I remember this used to be an old homestead. Weren't the outbuildings falling down in the fields? You really turned this place around."

"Thanks." Pride shone like a soft new light.

She'd worked hard, he realized. Sacrificed a lot of her time, her energy and her courage to build this place with her own hands. Not what a lot of women her age did. No, they were falling in love and planning weddings and enjoying all that a marriage brought. A home, maybe a new car or two, babies to welcome into the world and raise.

He hadn't known she'd literally built this place. It had to have been about the time Deb was diagnosed and his world fell apart. He hadn't noticed much in the way of anything after that. Woodenly doing his job to the best of his ability and hurrying home to her, to all that mattered to him.

Sadness crept into his heart, for Deb. For Kendra. That had to be around the time he'd handcuffed Jerrod. "Folks didn't criticize you for doing all this, did they? This is an incredible job."

"Thanks." She shrugged, turning away from him as if to hide her true emotions.

All he saw was Kendra, as she always looked, hair tied back neatly, shimmering in the sunlight, casual but looking impeccable in faded jeans and a shirt, scuffed riding boots and a leather belt cinched at her slim waist. A small gold cross glinted in the hollow between her collarbones.

Had she put all her heartache into this place? Working hard to forget, moving so far out of town for peace, for distance from anyone who could hurt her?

He knew something about heartbreak.

He could see the spread through the wide double doorway at the head of the stable. Perfect rail fencing, groomed paddocks, mellow green meadows, covered arenas, two other new stable buildings and the hint of the original brick cottage nestled behind two ancient maples.

A massive change from what this place used to look like—a forgotten, falling-down homestead that had sat unused, except for the grazing cattle and growing hay.

He'd always assumed she'd had the place rebuilt. She came from one of the area's wealthier families. She could probably pull together a loan for that kind of an investment. But to have done this herself?

He was real glad he'd chosen to go with her stable.

She ambled away from him. Her gait wasn't jaunty, but not slow, either. A graceful, quiet way she moved. Unconscious of her country-girl beauty. Looking so wholesome and good-hearted, she made him notice.

What are you trying to tell me, Lord? Puzzled, Cameron followed after the lovely lady who was affecting him.

"Come take a look," she invited, pausing in front of a stall with a horse in it.

The big animal made a low sound in its throat, nosing over the low gate to press its muzzle into Kendra's waiting hand. Nuzzling against her palm, sighing at the wonder of Kendra's caring touch. The horse closed its eyes in obvious bliss.

"This is one of my best friends, Willow." Kendra leaned her forehead against the horse's, their affection for one another clear.

As warm as sunlight and twice as dazzling, the woman before him changed. Her defenses falling, she looked better, brighter.

That horse looked awful big. Kendra was right. He also saw the bond between woman and horse. Friendship.

Yep. He could use some of that.

"Oh! Stop that, Sprite!" Kendra's reprimand was sprinkled with merriment as she whisked her ponytail out of another horse's mouth. "Stop being jealous."

"Your horse, too?" He'd seen her on one that looked sort of like that when she rode to town. From the shadows in the neighboring stall, he couldn't get a real good take on the color of the horse, except it was dark.

"Yeah. This is my barrel horse. We took first in the state last year, but I'm not competing anymore."

"I read about that in the local paper. Hometown girl does good."

She rolled her eyes. "Not so good. It's really the horse." She didn't know how to say it, but she was blessed to have these horse friends in her life.

"So, are these all your animals?" He gazed down the aisle at the other animals holding out for attention.

"Not the rest in this aisle. This is my best rental

stable. Nice big box stalls with attached corrals for them to stretch their legs during the day.''

"Looks like you've got a lot of space available."

"No, it's Saturday. Our busiest of the week. Kids come in to spend the day with their horses."

"Just kids?"

"Mostly, but about a third of my clients are adults. Lots of country girls like me, who grew up on a little land with room enough for a horse. They have to work in Bozeman where the jobs are and can't pasture a horse in a subdivision, so they board here. It's a good compromise."

"Looks like you do a good business."

"It's what I love." And what she knew. Horses were her life. She gave Sprite a snuggle before leading the way down the mostly empty aisle.

"Meet Jingles. She's an American quarter horse—" Kendra giggled as the horse lipped her cheek. She pulled a roll of spearmint candies out of her pocket and slipped the horse two.

Cameron watched in amazement as the horse crunched the hard candy into pieces. "She can eat that? It won't make her sick?"

"Jingles has a sweet tooth, just like her owner." Kendra stroked the mare's golden neck. "She's a great horse. The breed is smart, loyal and fast, has great endurance and good tempers. Can't be beat for saddle riding."

"I saw a few ads for quarter horses in the paper.

Sure is different seeing them up close. I remember they were pricey.''

''They can be.'' Kendra remembered how her parents had scrimped and saved to help her buy Jingles for her fourteenth birthday. She'd taken Jingles all the way to the state competitions and won, five years running, but it had been a sacrifice for her family, she remembered.

Cameron was looking for a new hobby to fill his leisure time, not a financial drain. And the look in his dark, steady gaze when he looked at the horses was nothing short of longing. He wanted this new life so badly, she could feel it.

He'd be awesome with a horse. It was easy to see. He had the right character—even tempered, level-headed and kind.

He had a lot to offer a horse. And the companionship a horse could give him, why, it would help ease the lonely hours he had to be facing.

She so wanted to find the right match for him. ''I promise we'll find something affordable. Have you figured out what you can spend?''

He shrugged. ''I'm flexible. I just don't want to buy something fancy when I'm more of a sensible sedan sort of guy.''

''No, not you.''

''Okay, a four-wheel drive, independent-suspension kind of man, but don't tell anyone. That would blow my shot at winning the election.''

''I can keep that secret…for a price.''

"Just add it to the tab I'm about to charge up."

He had a nice laugh, warm and deep like summer thunder over a mountain valley. Was it her imagination, or was she relaxing around him? She wasn't shaking and she'd forgotten to be wary.

What was that all about? She hadn't felt this safe being alone with a man who wasn't a member of her family for years. She spun on her heel and led the way through the blast of an industrial air-conditioning unit.

"C'mon back to my office," she called over her shoulder when he didn't follow her. "I've got price lists on everything you can expect to spend, from vet bills to the kind of tack you're going to need and what it will probably cost."

"Wow. That sure saves me a lot of research."

"It's good to know what you're getting into. I've made up brochures on everything you need to think about. If you're really going to do this, it's a bigger commitment than most people expect."

"The worthwhile relationships always are."

Was it her imagination, or did he sound as if he was hurting? It made her remember Gramma's words. Cancer is a hard enemy, she'd said. Was Cameron thinking about the wife he'd lost? It sounded as if he had been devoted to her, had cared for her through her illness.

What did they say about him? That he was a rare and devoted man. She ached for his loss.

It was a good thing he'd gotten up the courage to

ask her about finding a horse. She *so* wanted to help him. She shouldered through her door, ignored the pile of paperwork heaped on her secondhand desk and flipped through a drawer for the right brochures. "I'll give you my rental rates for the different horses. Rent—if you want to start riding lessons before we find your perfect mount."

"Wow." He bent to study the brochure, giving her a perfect view of a cowlick at the crown of his head.

Her stomach fluttered, and she knew it was that sense of rightness, when everything fell into place. She liked to think the work she did with her stable made a difference, however small in the world, for the people and children who came here.

By the look of hope on Cameron's face, lined by sun and hardship, she knew he would find happy hours ahead and the companionship he'd been needing.

He refolded the brochure and stuck it in his back jeans pocket. "I'm real sure about this. I've been giving it a lot of thought for some time."

"Good. When do you want to get started?"

"I've got time now." All of it lonely, so much of it that it hurt to think about too much. He pulled a quarter-folded section of newspaper from his back pocket and studied it. "I've circled a few ads that look good. What do you think?"

She bent close, taking the page he offered. The newsprint rattled as she studied it. Cameron dared to edge close enough to peer over her shoulder. He'd never stood so close to her before, and it was like being touched by spring. She smelled sweet like flowers.

She'd sure make a nice wife. Where did that thought come from? The realization filled him, steady like winter rain, when he ought to be paying attention to what she was saying. Her mouth was moving, he could hear the gentle alto of her words, but he couldn't focus.

His pulse drummed in his ears and seconds stretched long, the way they did when he was on the job, his Smith & Wesson drawn, adrenaline pumping and senses heightened.

There might not be a perp pulling a gun on him, but as he felt the silken graze of Kendra's hair against his jaw, he knew this moment was as pivotal.

Kendra must have realized stray strands of her hair had escaped her ponytail. Her hand brushed those wisps into place behind her dainty ear, where a small diamond winked on her earlobe.

She liked jewelry, he realized, something he'd never noticed before. The necklace, the tasteful set of pierced earrings and a small ruby ring on her right hand.

"I know this person, and no, this isn't a good deal. Basically, she's wanting what a luxury sedan would bring in when what she really has is a base-model economy car."

"I like a woman who uses terms I can understand."

He was rewarded with her gentle smile. "This one's a student of mine. Her mare is a nice midsize car at a reasonable market price. She's one aisle over, if you want to go take a look at her.''

"I'm here. Might as well.'' He tried to sound casual, as if it was no big deal.

No, this was *huge*. It had been tough coming to the place in his life where he'd finished grieving, hard to let go and accept that he still had a life. And that Deb, the angel she surely was, would want him to live and not just put one foot in front of the other, sleepwalking through life.

Life was a finite gift. He'd learned how important it was to spend this time on earth wisely, with love and purpose. That was why he was here now, following Kendra through the stable and into the bright light of day.

This was one thing of about a million that she loved about her work. Helping bring a deserving horse and rider together. And in Cameron's case, it felt like a personal mission as she arrowed through the sunny grounds, waving to kids on their horses calling out her name.

"Are those kids you found horses for?''

"No, kids I taught to ride.''

"Cool.'' His boots crunched in the gravel next to her. "Do you teach all the riding classes?''

"About half of them.''

No matter how fast she walked, he stayed right there at her side. This was business, and showing Cameron around was no different than the hundreds of other times she'd done this with other potential boarders.

Why was she more aware of the sound of his gait, confident and strong and slightly uneven? Had he been wounded in the line of duty? He might be casually dressed in a T-shirt and jeans instead of his navy-blue uniform, but there was no way on this earth she could forget he was a sheriff.

She turned cold inside and refused to let the next thoughts come. Or the memories of a time she needed to forget and never think of again.

Could a person bury memories forever? She was going to give it her best shot. What mattered was this life she'd built, the kids practicing their riding skills in the different arenas or paddocks. The giggling girls in groups of two or three that rode off on the manicured trails.

This was her life. Think about that, Kendra.

"This is the riding arena." The covered, open-air area was fenced with riser seating on the far side. "We do our Western training and competitions here."

"I see the barrels." He squinted, gesturing to where a white mare dug into a tight corner around the final barrel, kicking up dust on her ride home. "Is that the horse?"

"That's her. She's a pleasure to ride."

"She looks too fancy for me."

"She's well priced, but she's trained for competition." How could she be so dense? "I never asked what type of riding you wanted to do."

"The sheriff over at Moose Creek is a good friend of mine. He's a horseman and takes his mount out in the mountains to hunt and fish. Says there's nothing like riding trails to get away from it all."

"He's right. That's what you'd like? A horse to trail ride with?"

"I used to head out into the mountains all the time. Hiking, skiing, fishing, hunting, camping. Then Deb got sick and everything changed."

Life could be so unfair sometimes. Kendra didn't have to ask if he'd had a happy marriage. It was in his voice, on his face, in his stance.

"Hey, Kendra." Susan, the rider on the white mare, headed over. "I noticed you two checking out my horse. Are you thinking about buying?"

"He's just starting to look." Kendra leaned her forearms on the top rail of the board fence, glad to see one of her oldest friends. "You know Cameron, right?"

"Sure." Susan gave Cameron her best smile. "Not here to give any of us a ticket, are you, Sheriff?"

"Nope. Off duty today." He offered his hand to the horse and let the mare scent his palm.

There was something about the man's hands. Something rare and striking. They were strong and square with broad palms and long, thick-knuckled fingers. His skin was bronzed by a summer spent out of doors and dusted with a trace of dark hair. Hands that looked brawny enough to break bones.

His tenderness was unexpected as he stroked the

mare's velvety nose. The mare responded with a friendly nicker deep in her throat. Kendra watched, astonished, as before her eyes Cameron's tough-guy shield fell away, the only face of this man she'd ever seen.

Standing before her, graced by the vivid sun, the real Cameron Durango was revealed. His integrity of steel. His caring nature. His excruciating loneliness.

As the lucky mare nickered again, nudging his hand for more attention, Kendra realized she wasn't afraid around him, not any longer.

She felt safe with him, because look at him. He was a truly good man. Hard lines cut into the corners of his eyes and around his mouth. Put there by hardship and worry and sadness. By grief she couldn't begin to compare hers with.

How could she not like him? He was lonely, and she knew something about that. She'd do her very best to find him the right horse. The friend he was looking to make.

He looked over his glasses at the woman in the saddle. ''Why are you selling her?''

''Financial problems.''

What was her name? Susan? She'd been a few years behind him in school—and sure looked sad about having to sell her horse.

He supposed it was easy to become attached. It was just as well he didn't want such a…a *woman's* horse. ''She's way too fancy for the likes of me.''

Susan looked relieved. "Kendra, I'll stable her myself."

"No problem." Kendra shrugged, waving off some unspoken concern with one slim hand.

She obviously ran a healthy business here. The girls clinging to the backs of their big horses ringed the arena, taking turns at the barrels or, in the corner, waiting for the comments of a woman instructor.

It was clear that Kendra was a good businesswoman, but she wasn't ruthless. He hadn't thought she was, or he wouldn't be standing here, but it was reassuring to see.

"If you want to wait a few minutes until Colleen is done with her class…" Kendra said without looking at him, taking great interest in how the class across the way was going. "It's too bad I have a class in a few minutes, or I'd personally stay to show you some of our trails."

What? "You're sending me out in the mountains with a stranger?"

"Don't worry, Colleen has all her shots."

He liked a woman with a sense of humor. "I'm glad to know that, but my big worry is you. You don't invite greenhorns like me out here, do you, and play practical jokes on them?"

"It's tempting, but I won't put you on the back of a wild horse and abandon you."

"Whew. I was worried."

"You look it. You have a suspicious nature, Sheriff."

"Just because I'm suspicious doesn't mean they aren't after me."

"That's paranoid, not suspicious."

"I knew that didn't sound right. Say, how long are your classes? I don't mind hanging around until you're done. I've got nothing else to do."

Kendra waved at the instructor from the class in the far corner that was disbanding.

Maybe he ought to be insulted Kendra was trying hard to get rid of him. She was probably busy, and he *had* taken up a chunk of her time. Why did he feel disappointed at the idea of her leaving him?

At first he barely noticed the brunette approaching on horseback. She drew her horse to a stop, studied them both and couldn't hide the big grin on her face. "Whew, what brings you out here, Sheriff? It's nothing serious, right?"

Kendra spoke up. "Cameron here is thinking about buying a horse and boarding here."

"Well, don't let me get in the way of business." The instructor tossed Kendra a secret look. "I don't mind taking the last class of the day for you. I could use the extra hours if you want to take the sheriff into the hills."

As if mulling it over, Kendra blew out a breath, ruffling her wispy bangs. "Fine by me. That is, if the sheriff can stand more of my company."

"I've suffered through worse."

"Me, too." Trouble twinkled in her eyes. "That

only leaves one question, cowboy. Are you ready to ride?''

"Sure thing. I'm up for the challenge."

Her smile was like heavenly light, warming him to the soul, as she spun away on the heel of her scuffed riding boots, calling out to someone just out of sight in the stable. Why did it feel as if she were taking his heart with her?

Chapter Five

Kendra gave the cinch a hard tug and tightened the buckle a notch. She always did her best not to be alone with any of the men who'd come her way, in a business sense. She'd gotten very practiced at it, but apparently not practiced enough because she was alone with Cameron.

Well, not *alone,* exactly, considering there were about fifty people around within calling distance. But soon they would be.

This is business, she reminded herself firmly. She was safe with Cameron. Not only that, but it felt like divine intervention, somehow. As if she was the one who could best help him find the right horse and a new, rewarding hobby to fill his time.

The horses in her life had certainly made hers fulfilling.

The old gelding she was saddling waited patiently

as she gave the cinch a final tug. One of the first horses she'd gotten for her ranch and her best beginner-class horse.

"You're a good gentleman, Palouse." Kendra patted the gray roan, his dappled coat and his white mane a throwback to his wild mustang heritage, and let him nuzzle her gloved hand affectionately. She slipped him a peppermint.

"I see you're a tough master." Cameron ambled close, planted his fists. "Do the animal-control people know about you?"

"They sure do. I'm on the top of their list to bring recovered horses to."

"Suppose I should have guessed that before I tried to tease. Horses must be abused, like any animal can be."

Or person, Kendra didn't add. "It certainly isn't the animal's fault. Horses need to trust their owners one hundred percent. They want to trust. They are loving creatures that don't deserve harsh treatment. I've rehabilitated about a dozen horses. Palouse was one of them."

"You'd never know it. He's as calm as could be. You must have done wonders with him."

"He's the wonder. You wait until you get to know more horses, then you'll know what I'm talking about. They are special blessings, and to share trust and love with them is a privilege."

There was no mistaking the big gelding's trust in her as he watched her with an adoring gaze.

That said a lot about the woman, in Cam's opinion. Professionally and personally.

"I've got Palouse saddled. How about you, are you ready to go?" She gathered the long leather straps of the reins.

As if he knew what to do with those. "Are you sure he'll go easy on me?"

"He's one of the gentlest horses I know. Six-year-olds learn to ride on him."

"I'm well past six, so I reckon I can handle him."

"That's the attitude I like to hear. Just put your foot in this stirrup and grab the saddle horn. Give a little hop and lift up into the saddle. Like this."

She demonstrated, rising up so she stood straight in the stirrup, her weight balanced on her one foot as if she were born to do it. "Ease your leg over his back, careful not to scrape him with your boot and settle into the seat. Don't let your weight drop, just lower your fanny into the saddle."

"I can do that. I've watched enough westerns, I ought to be able to ride by osmosis."

"Fine, then mount up, could you?"

"Sure thing, little lady."

Kendra held the stirrup steady when he had trouble catching it with the toe of his boot. Just as she'd do for any new student taking his first ride.

Why did she feel different? It was as if something was buzzing around her, like the charge in the air before a thunderstorm.

But the skies were clear to the west and to the south, where summer storms often started.

It was Cameron. He seemed to take up all the empty space around her, although it made no sense. She could smell the clean woodsy scent of him and hear the creak of leather as he stepped into the stirrup. Muscles corded beneath his sun-bronzed forearms as he rose into the saddle, casting his shadow over her.

How could she not be aware of him? Of his power? Of his striking male presence? She didn't want to trust any man again, but that didn't mean she was immune to a good man's appeal. It only proved she should have paid Colleen to take Cameron around instead of taking over the class.

Why hadn't she? It didn't make any sense. What was the difference if Colleen was paid for an extra hour on the trail or in the arena? Why hadn't Kendra thought of that at the time?

Because there was obviously something wrong with her brain whenever the handsome sheriff was around, that's why. As if her synapses misfired. How else could she explain it? First, she let him repair her trailer tire—*not* what she'd let any man other than her brother-in-law do. Now she was riding out with Cameron.

Hadn't she learned enough lessons from Jerrod?

Yes. She might be *aware* of Cameron but that didn't mean she was *interested* in him. It was something that could never be. The barricade around her heart was impenetrable and was going to stay that way.

She slipped Jingles a peppermint from her jeans pocket and pressed her forehead to the mare's sun-warmed neck. The comforting scent of horse eased away the worries knotted in Kendra's stomach.

Tension eased from the back of her neck as Jingles cuddled back, leaning against Kendra's body in unspoken affection. As if the mare was telling her, *You're not alone. I'm here. You can count on me.*

"And you can count on me, friend," Kendra whispered, tracing her hand through the mare's platinum mane. "Let's go for a ride."

Jingles stomped impatiently, and Kendra didn't look at the man watching her as she hiked up into the saddle and reined the mare around. Why did she feel Cameron's presence as tangibly as the heat of the sun on her face?

She demonstrated how to hold the reins in one hand, and leaned over to make sure there was enough slack in the straps he held. "Palouse knows to follow me. Just keep the reins at the saddle horn, easy like this. Don't jerk them and don't kick him."

"So basically I just sit here."

"Yep. Palouse knows what he's doing, so you can just enjoy your first ride. Just trust him and enjoy the view."

"I thought horses could be unpredictable."

"They can be, but Palouse is eighteen. That's pretty old for a horse. This graybeard's seen just about everything, and he knows his job. He takes it seriously. He'll take good care of you, if you're kind to him. That's the way it works best in the horse world.''

''Know what? The ground *does* look a long way down from up here.''

''And it's hard when you hit.''

''You're teasing me, right?''

''Sure. Yep. Just teasing you.''

She took off ahead of him, and the big horse lumbered into motion beneath him, scaring him near to death because it just didn't feel right. He was going to tip out of the saddle. He had some real concerns, the ground *did* look like it was uncomfortable to land on.

And was he thinking about falling to his death? No, he was watching Kendra. He was noticing the sparkling warmth within her.

The horse beneath him picked up speed as they strolled through the stable yard, his gait an unsettling rocking and swaying that was likely to make Cam seasick. Either that, or he was going to lose his balance and fall like a klutz into the gravel.

He was an athletic man and an outdoorsman, and he liked every outdoor activity he'd ever tried. Except this. This was *not* like pedaling a bike or zipping down a hillside on a motorcycle. He wasn't in control, and he didn't know if he liked it.

You've got two choices, man. Abandon your plan, or go ahead with it.

Maybe he would learn to love riding horses. Although that probability was growing smaller as time passed. The seasick feeling was getting worse with the way the horse was rocking forward and back, and Cam was sitting up on top like a tiny boat on a rolling ocean. Yep, that's what this reminded him of. The ground swayed beneath him.

People called this fun?

His stomach clenched like a fist. He wasn't going to get sick, right? In front of Kendra? *That* would be real attractive. She'd certainly never look at him again in the same light.

If it's not too much trouble, Lord, please get me through this. I'll tough it out, I promise. Just a little help would be appreciated.

"This is why I had to have this property." Kendra's soft alto, as gentle as spring rain, caught his attention. Made him look up and notice that the golden fields of her horse ranch had fallen behind them and they'd crossed into the tree line.

They were surrounded by sparse lodgepole pine, cedar and fir. The evergreens clung to the stubborn earth with tenacious roots, their branches spread wide to catch the sun. The trees were scattered, casting shadows across the open ground between them.

He forgot to feel sick taking in the awesome beauty of the rising foothills, the towering amethyst peaks of the Bridger Range ahead and the true blue of the Montana sky above. But such beauty seemed fleeting when Kendra pulled back her sleek golden mare so they were side by side.

Her Stetson cut a jaunty angle to block the sun's glare. She studied him from under the gray brim. "Don't you love this?"

"What's not to love?" He could learn to like feeling seasick.

She apparently wasn't fooled as she squinted, studying him. Did he look as green as he felt?

"Do you want to head back?"

That would mean his time would be over. That was *not* what he wanted. No way.

He would stick it out, whether he survived it or not. "I'm likin' this well enough."

"I think you're lying." Her eyes twinkled.

"Yeah, but I *will* like this. Once I get the hang of it. It's kind of like riding a canoe upside down in an ocean."

"At least there's no storm swells."

"True. No hurricanes."

"No waterspouts, whirlpools or tidal waves. See? Riding is pretty tame compared to other sports."

"Like what sports? High-altitude parachuting? Free rock climbing?" He gave thanks they'd come to a swaying stop. "You ought to smile more often, Miss McKaslin."

"I smile all the time."

"You smile about as often as I do."

Cameron had a whole lot more to be sad about, in her opinion, than she ever would. No, the Lord had been generous with all His blessings in her life. But Cameron…

She shut off the image of him taking care of an ill woman, bringing her meals, tucking the blankets beneath her chin and reading to her in the soft glow of a small lamp. She knew he'd cared for his wife like that, because she'd seen the tenderness in him when he'd patted Palouse's neck. The goodness shone in him like the sun, radiant and unmistakable and genuine.

Time for a subject change. The more of a hero she made Cameron Durango, the harder it was going to be to keep her shields up full force.

Business. This is about business, Kendra. Stop forgetting that! She nosed Jingles into motion along the groomed trail, between the sweep of fir boughs and the call of a red-tailed hawk overhead.

"We offer over forty acres of riding trails on-site, and national forest borders one side of my property. There are miles of old logging-road trails, although it's not the best time of year to go wandering up into the mountains alone."

"I suppose that's what those ropes across the trail ahead would mean."

"Exactly, but we'll ride around them. I think we're both experienced enough to handle any wilderness situation."

"I'm armed, if that helps."

"Am I that dangerous, Sheriff?"

"Maybe," he quipped. "No, I'm the only sheriff in these parts. When I'm off duty, I'm still on call."

"You want to keep going?" Her question was gently spoken, but it was a challenge.

He couldn't resist a good challenge. "You lead the way. I'll follow."

"Here's a hint. Don't look down, okay? You'll do a lot better. C'mon. I promise, you'll like what you see if you just stick with it."

He already did. She balanced ahead of him on that golden horse of hers, riding into the long rays of light arrowing through the trees, her blond hair whipping behind her.

The horse lurched forward beneath him. Cameron swallowed. Don't look down? Then he'd keep his gaze on her. Fir boughs brushed his knees and his elbows as he followed her. He wouldn't think about the narrow path the horse was now following, or that it fell away into nothing, except for the sturdy split-rail guard that stood between him and the hereafter.

"You let kids ride on this?"

"Trail safety is part of the lessons they take. You aren't afraid of heights, are you, Sheriff?"

"No. Heights don't bug me. Falling hard and breaking a few bones does."

"It isn't a far drop, and the trail is as wide as a road. Horses are surefooted. You're perfectly safe. What do you think of the view?"

He'd forgotten to look around him. He'd been so busy watching her. Watching the graceful arch of her neck, the delicate cut of her shoulders. The hint of her shoulder blades against the soft white knit shirt she wore.

The golden shimmer of her hair, caught back in a white scrunch thing at the base of her neck, shivered over her shoulder as she glanced back at him.

"When I first viewed this property, I was disappointed. The outbuildings were so run-down, useless, and the house hadn't been lived in for twenty years. But the moment Jingles and I set out here up this trail, I knew I'd come home. Look."

They curved around a granite outcropping and the rough amethyst peaks of the Bridger Range speared into a sky close enough to touch. The rugged foothills of meadows and trees spread out around them, climbing upward, as if in reverence to the mountains.

"God's handiwork sure is something." It was all he could think of to say.

"Exactly. Forty acres of this is mine. Mostly wilderness except for the manicured trails. I know, because I made those trails myself."

He shouldn't have been surprised, not after she'd admitted to learning better than adequate carpenter skills. "When did you buy this property?"

"About six years ago."

That explained it. Right after he'd rescued her that day. Right after he'd driven her to the hospital. Sorrow for her banded his chest like a vise.

Had she put all her heartbreak and all her broken dreams into this place? "Must have been difficult clearing these paths."

"It took me most of four months working every afternoon until dusk. I got pretty good with an ax, a saw and a shovel."

"You did all the railing, too?"

"Until my blisters had blisters."

Forty acres of trails? It had to have taken the better part of a year. How could someone so small and delicate work that hard?

Heartbreak. He knew, because that's how it had been after Deb passed. He'd worked long hours taking up the slack of being a single officer in a growing district, until the city had hired a deputy. He hadn't realized how much he'd stayed at the office, doing paperwork well into the evening until Frank had shown up to help out.

Only then had Cam been aware of the aching emptiness in his life.

Yeah, he knew what Kendra was talking about. He took in the rustic trails, groomed so they blended well with the environment, and the carefully constructed wooden rails that marked the edges of the trails. Solidly made.

This is where Kendra had put all her broken dreams.

It took a lot of guts to put your life back together. He admired her more as the horse moved beneath him, obediently following Kendra.

This isn't so bad, he realized. There was a sort of rhythm to the horse's gait, and he was starting to get the knack of this riding thing. At least he didn't feel seasick anymore.

He breathed deep, taking in the beauty of the day. A strange weightless feeling expanded in his chest. Something he hadn't felt in more years than he could count—happiness.

He wanted to remember this forever. How the clean mountain air smelled like summer and sage and pine needles. The rustle of the wind in the bear grass. The faint *thunk* of hooves on the hard-packed earth. The creak of the leather saddle beneath him. The sense of rightness—as if heaven were smiling down on them in approval.

"Look, there's a fawn. He's still got his spots." Kendra whispered, her horse stopping in the middle of the trail. "Do you see him?"

Branches swayed peacefully to his left. If he squinted, Cam could make out the faint outline of a doe frozen in the underbrush, ears alert, soft eyes unblinking, tensed as if ready to flee. At her side was a fragile, knobby-kneed fawn.

They were within throwing distance. Too close for a wild animal's comfort, surely, but instead of streaking off and taking her baby with her, the doe blinked, watching Kendra.

"You must ride up here a lot." He pitched his voice low, to keep from scaring off the deer. "She's used to you."

"Sure she is. Wildlife comes down into the foothills to feed this time of year, when the mountains get so dry. After I bed the horses for the night, I go out and leave some hay and grain in the feed troughs for them. She's probably one of the deer that waits for me every evening. When they know you're not hunting them but bringing them grain, they get pretty bold.''

"Do they come right up to you?''

"Within a few feet.''

If he were a deer, he'd come up to her, too. Her gentle voice and radiant kindness were unmistakable. He had no problem picturing her feeding the wildlife. Not as many landowners in these parts would be so generous. Wild animals were seen as nuisances, mostly. And often dangerous.

As delicate and willowy as Kendra looked, she had confidence, too. She was capable. She knew how to take care of herself in the backcountry. He guessed the small pack tied to the side of her saddle, hardly noticeable, held necessities like a hand radio, knives, snakebite kit and maybe a small handgun. It looked just the right size for all that.

"I get mostly deer, elk and a few moose. The deer are the most frequent. They show up every evening and lay around the house on my lawn to sleep. I had to put up ten-foot lattice all around my rose garden to keep them out.''

"I take it they eat roses?''

"Oh, do they. The first summer I was here, they ate my tea roses down to the stems. Let's leave mama and baby. I saw some moose up here just yesterday. Maybe we can spot them again.''

"Suppose you see more dangerous critters up here, too."

"Sometimes."

The path had turned steep and rocky, but Kendra didn't seem worried as her surefooted mare curved around the steep hillside toward mountains so close, he had to tip his head back to see their granite faces.

"Sometimes? That doesn't sound reassuring."

"I've come across everything from rattlers to bears."

"And lived to tell the tale, huh?" He hadn't guessed she'd like the backcountry, too. A lot of women preferred shopping malls to spending a day where wolves and bears hunted.

"Mostly I mind my own business, they mind theirs. But that's why I keep the riders down below the tree line this time of year. So they're safe."

They'd risen so high and fast up the slope, he couldn't see her ranch below, just the far edge of the extensive valley stretching out behind him in gold and green.

"Want to head back?"

She'd noticed where he was looking. "Back? No, I was just taking in the view. You can see the Rockies from here. And the Tobacco Roots."

"Can you imagine when all this was wilderness, before the settlers came from the East in their wagons?"

"It had to look like this. Except *wilder*." Lewis and Clark had come this way in their canoe and crossed on foot the rest of the way, over the Great Divide. "Clark wrote of seeing nothing but giant herds of elk and deer and buffalo for miles."

"It's amazing to think that it's still the same wilderness, isn't it? Without the giant herds."

"That what I love about heading up into the backcountry. It's finding that part of Montana that's wild. The way it was a hundred years ago."

"Exactly."

How weird that he felt that, too. Kendra didn't know how to explain it, just that she was aware of the past that had come before her, in the hunting pair of eagles overhead and the peaceful deer resting in the undergrowth or the quiet reverence of an old-growth pine grove that had clung to the side of the mountains when natives hunted and cared for their families and each other.

God's handiwork was timeless.

They rode in companionable silence for a long while, until the sun touched the tops of the trees, making long shadows in the bunches of wildflowers and bear grass.

When she heard the faint rush and gurgle of running water, she guided Jingles off the beaten path and through the shade of Douglas fir. Creek water trickled over smooth, round rocks, so clear and clean it sparkled like diamonds in the sunlight.

"My favorite picnic spot. Just Jingles and I know about it."

"Not anymore."

"I guess I can share this place with you, since you understand." She let the reins slide through her fingers, giving her mare enough slack to sip from the fresh cool water.

Palouse came to a rocking stop and did the same.

Wow. This was going better than he'd ever thought. He leaned on the wide shelf below the saddle horn, the way he'd seen his heroes Clint and John do.

What should he say now? No witty banter came to mind. Think, man. He felt itchy. Antsy. Why?

"Look, fresh tracks." Kendra swung nimbly out of the saddle.

Okay, that was why. Were they in danger? "I don't think that's a good idea, getting down like that." They were cougar prints. He could see them plain as day at the edge of the creek, beginning to fill in with water. "The cat was just here."

"Still is." Kneeling, Kendra nodded toward the way they'd come. Calm, quiet, not moving.

That was good. Never a smart idea to act like panicked prey in the backcountry. He eased down slow, glad for the locked and loaded Smith & Wesson on his hip.

"I've never had one threaten me. Mostly they keep their distance. Look, there she is. Under the fir branch there against the bank, crouched low. Oh, she's pretty."

Cam couldn't spot the animal from where he was, and he didn't like that. The back of his neck prickled.

He liked to keep an eye on his enemies, assuming the mountain lion was looking for an early supper.

Then he saw it, a second before the low fir boughs shivered. He had his gun in his hand and was on his feet in front of Kendra, ready to protect her with his life.

The golden brown blur slipped soundlessly away over the carpet of the forest. The branches shivered, and the next instant there was no trace of the predator. Adrenaline kicked in, thrumming through him until he could hardly breathe.

He'd been so rattled, so fierce with the need to protect her, that he wasn't thinking straight. He was a tracker. He could see plain as day the cougar hadn't been hunting. Now he felt like a fool and reholstered his revolver.

"Awesome." Unaware, Kendra rose gracefully and handed him a small bottle of water from her small nylon saddle pack and kept one for her.

"You were going to protect me." She sounded amazed as she removed the plastic lid with a supple twist of her wrist and took a long pull.

"You? No, I was worried about *me*. I didn't want to be that cougar's early supper."

"You have a real protective vibe going, don't you, Sheriff?"

Did he look as embarrassed as he felt? "Part of my job. Habit."

"Habit? Like how you serve and protect?"

"Hey, don't go thinking I'm noble or something,

because I'm not." How was he going to talk his way out of this one?

"Oh?" She crooked one eyebrow, not fooled.

"I was protecting my best interests. You know the buddy rule?"

"Sure. Don't go into the woods alone, so you have someone to help if you need it."

"Sure, but there's more to it than that. I always make sure I go with a slower runner, that way if a bear or a cougar takes after us, you'd be the first one they'd catch and I'd be just fine."

"That's a fine plan, but guess what? How do you know that I'm a slower runner than you are? That's why *I* wanted to take you out here instead of Colleen. She's a really slow runner, and I'd hate to lose another employee. They take time to train. You, on the other hand, what's another boarder? They're a dime a dozen."

"You'd let a bear eat me, huh?"

"Absolutely. About as easily as you'd let a bear attack me."

She couldn't remember when she'd laughed with a man like this since Jerrod. It just went to show what a decent man Cameron was. He'd jumped to protect her, physically put himself in harm's way for her sake. Without a thought. He just did it.

Just as he'd done before.

The laughter inside her vanished.

She retrieved her reins, fighting to keep from remembering that night. The scent of cooled sausage-

and-olive pizza sitting on the kitchen table. The rhythm of rain beating the aluminum siding. Thunder crashing overhead as if the night were breaking apart around her. Cameron pounding at the door, the flash of red-and-blue strobes cutting through the closed slats of the plastic window blinds—

"Are we heading back?" He sounded disappointed.

She gathered her reins, keeping her back to him so he couldn't see her shivering or the goose bumps on her arms, even as the bold sun scorched her skin.

He mounted up clumsily, but good for a second attempt. "Know what I think?"

Kendra found herself in the saddle, reins gathered, turning Jingles away from the creek and toward the trail. Toward home. She wanted to go home.

"I like this. It's peaceful. It's closer to being like hiking than I thought it would be. Not as near to the ground."

She nodded, acknowledging his attempt at humor.

"It's peaceful. Closer to nature, something you don't get on a motorbike or four-wheeling."

A tip of a pine bough brushed against her cheek, startling her. Reminding her where she was. She was here, safe, the memories were gone, tucked safely away behind the shields protecting her heart. Leaving a growing emptiness.

An emptiness that had swallowed all the warmth and laughter she'd felt with Cameron. That left her feeling alone, as she was meant to be.

She stayed several yards ahead of Cameron on the return trip through the tree line and along the well-used path until the fields and the paddocks and the buildings came into sight.

Chapter Six

Kendra couldn't resist standing at her new niece's crib for a few more moments, gazing down on the sleeping infant, so sweet and precious and new. Love shone like the sun inside her heart. Gramma's words came to mind. *That's what your little girl will look like one day.*

No way, Gramma. Kendra brushed her hand over the infant's downy head, her fine hair already thicker and curlier than when she'd been born. She was a McKaslin, all right, with the gold locks.

"You look like your mom, not me," she told the baby, who sighed in her sleep, pressing into Kendra's touch.

Oh, I'm going to spoil you rotten, little girl. It was an aunt's privilege, after all. She thought of all the birthday presents to buy, all the fun outings ahead, finding her first pony and teaching her to ride. Buying her riding boots and her first cowboy hat. So much to look forward to.

She felt a tug on the hem of her denim shorts.

"Auntie Kendwa?" A big girl, two and a half years old, Allie stretched out both adorably chubby hands. "Up!"

"Hey, princess." Kendra settled her niece against her hip, heading for the door. "Are you up from your nap already?"

"Mine!" Allie pointed to the baby in the crib.

"That's right. She's your little sister. Isn't she nice?"

Allie nodded, her silken gold hair as soft as silk against Kendra's jaw. She smelled of baby shampoo and the laundry detergent Karen used and that sweet little-girl scent that was everything good. "Allie want cookie."

"Are you a hungry girl?"

A very serious nod. "Hungwy."

"Then we'd better go downstairs and check out the cookie jar. There just might be chocolate cookies."

"Yum."

Thoroughly charmed, Kendra started down the stairs and onto the main floor, careful to be quiet as she circled past the living room, where Karen was stretched out napping on the couch. She didn't stir.

"Cookie! Cookie!" Allie clapped her hands together, steepling her little fingers when she saw the jar had been refilled, thanks to a late-night baking.

"You can have two." Kendra handed one to the girl, who took a big bite and chewed happily.

She slipped Allie into her high chair, buckled her up and locked the tray in place. She left the second cookie within reach while she searched through the cupboard for a cup. When she turned around, Allie had a cookie in each hand, both missing a big bite out of the tops of them.

Too cute. Kendra felt her self-protective armor settle back in place. This is *not* what it would be like if she had a family of her own—she wasn't going to think like that. She wasn't ever going to go there. To start picturing in her mind what it would be like if she could find a man to trust.

A man like Cameron. The thought breezed into her mind so fast and stealthily, she couldn't stop it. And where had that come from? She was *far* from interested in the local sheriff. Really. She was fine all by herself. Just fine.

A light tap on the screen door had Allie squealing. "Gwamma! Gwamma!"

"Yes, it's me, little darling." Gramma slipped into the kitchen, carrying an insulated casserole dish and a rolled grocery bag on top, which she set on the edge of the kitchen island. "I brought dinner for you girls. I know, you were going to handle it, but you've been doing so much lately, I couldn't help wanting to pitch in."

"Thank you, Gramma." Kendra kissed her grandmother's soft cheek, as delicate as paper. "You look snazzy. Where are you off to with your boyfriend?"

"Imagine, a boyfriend at my age." Gramma sparkled with happiness as she pulled a small stuffed tiger from her purse, heading straight for the high chair and the little girl who was clapping in glee. "Look what Gramma got you."

"A kitty!" Chocolate ringed Allie's mouth and crumbs rained from her fingers as she reached out to claim her new toy.

"There's a concert over at the university," Gramma explained while Kendra poured Allie's milk. "Selections from Chopin. You know how I love classical music. Willard is spoiling me."

"I knew I liked that man." Kendra was glad to see that her grandmother, after being a widow for so long, had found someone who made her happy.

Please, help him to continue, she prayed. She worried about her gramma, who was so trusting. Sometimes it wasn't easy to see what lurked hidden inside a person—a man.

Isn't that how she'd felt about Jerrod? He'd been a truly wonderful boyfriend at first. And then—

Her stomach turned to ice and her hand shook. The spill-proof lid skidded through her fingers and milk sloshed over the rim.

"I'm glad you're taking your time getting to know Willard." She grabbed a paper towel to wipe up the mess. "It's good to go slow."

"I'm enjoying every moment. It's shameful how he

spoils me. I tell him so, too, but do you know what he says? Get used to it, Helen. Goodness. He's all but swept me off my feet.''

"It's good to keep your feet on the ground.''

"That's sensible advice from a woman who has never truly been in love.'' Gramma took the lid and snapped it into place. "True love is worth the flight and the fall. It's the journey that matters, dear. What choices we make, to love and to live, especially after we get hurt. Love is never a mistake. Remember that.''

Yes, it is. What else could Jerrod have been but a mistake? Maybe she'd been blind, but Jerrod had seemed kind and gallant at first. With everything she was and everything she had in her soul to give, she'd *wanted* to fall in love.

And she had. She'd been wrong. She'd made one huge glaring mistake, just one.

Nothing would ever be the same again. Nothing would ever be right.

"Great-Gramma loves you, darling.''

Kendra watched as her grandmother kissed the top of Allie's golden head, all curls and silk.

"I think it's great you're helping the sheriff out.'' Gramma flashed Kendra a knowing look. "He told me all about it when he came in for coffee this morning. Said how you were helping him find the right horse.''

"It is my job.''

"Exactly.'' Sparkling, full of hope, Gramma headed to the door in a swirl of color and beauty. "I'm so pleased you do your job well. Keep up the good work.''

Really. Kendra rolled her eyes. "You could mind your own business.''

"What fun would that be? Oh, hi, girls. I'm on my way out. Michelle, you're glowing. Kirby, you look pale. Are you getting enough sleep?''

"I had a late call last night," replied Kirby, the nurse, as she held the door. "Have a good time, Gramma.''

"Yeah, and behave!" Michelle called out, teasing. "I'm not sure about that grandmother of ours. Out until all hours of the evening with that boyfriend of hers.''

"The literature professor." Kirby, a year younger than Kendra, set the board game and the foil-covered cake pan on the table. "Are you ready for game night? I made chocolate cake.''

"Is that taco cheese-and-macaroni casserole I smell?" Michelle followed her nose to the counter. "Ooh, and Gramma's homemade rolls. We're eatin' good tonight, but not as good as little Allie.''

"Hello, cutie pie." Kirby freed their niece from the high chair. "Where's your mommy?''

"Sleeping," Kendra supplied while she preheated the oven. "You guys watch Allie for me, and I'll get supper on for us.''

"My pleasure." Kirby spirited their niece away.

Leaving Michelle to lean against the counter and gloat. "Do you know what I heard? That you spent yesterday afternoon with a certain handsome lawman. One that was the recipient of your baked goods the other day.''

"You mean Frank, the deputy?''

Michelle scowled playfully, because there was an abiding love between them. "Cameron is a good man. Good in the way that matters. The kind of man that stands tall and loves deep. Way to go, sis.''

"I'm not seeing the sheriff.''

"Face it. You literally *saw* him. You were alone with him. I'd call that a date.''

Her stomach turned into a cold, hard ball. "You're making something out of nothing. It's business. He wants to buy a horse. I'm going to help him. I do that. I own a riding stable, remember?''

"Yeah, but it doesn't have to be *all* business.'' Michelle grabbed the board game and began unboxing the set. The clatter of tokens and the spill of hotels filled the silence between them.

Kendra took the lettuce from the refrigerator and tore open the plastic wrap. Why were her hands trembling again? It's just business, she wanted to say one more time convincingly, but to who? To Michelle? Or herself?

Cameron is a good man. Good in the way that matters. How did Michelle know? And were there any good, decent men left out there? The kind that never hurt, that always stayed? How would she know when she found one?

Or would she make the same mistake?

As if in answer, her arm ached, the pins and plates that had held her bones together gone now, but the memory remained.

As deep as those scars had gone, there were others that had cut more deeply. Those scars hurt, too.

It was amazing the difference a new interest could make in a man's life. Cameron had slept like the dead, something he hadn't done in more years than he could count.

Rested, it was that much easier to face work on a Monday morning, whistling while he strolled around the echoing office making coffee and punching out reports.

Frank happened by a few minutes before eight o'clock, keys jingling, looking dog tired. "What's with you? I could toss you in the holding cell. There ought to be some ordinance against being happy before coffee."

"I've already had mine. It's hot." He gestured toward the low filing cabinet where the coffeemaker sat, light on, coffee steaming.

Frank frowned and he grabbed a mug with a clink and poured. "It's got to be that woman. If you're dating her, then does that mean we'll be getting more cookies?"

"You can hope, but I'm not dating her."

Frank swiped one of the last two from the plate by the sugar packets. "Want the last one?"

"Already helped myself." Cameron stapled the last

report and checked his e-mail. Nothing much, just a reminder for this month's council meeting from the mayor's secretary.

"Hmm, these sure are good." Frank chewed as he headed toward the door. "Did you score another date with her for this weekend?"

"I told you. I didn't have a first date with her."

"That's your story. I don't think you're telling me the truth, man."

"That's none of your business."

"Sure it is, if cookies are involved."

"We didn't have a date, but I did spend time with the lovely lady over the weekend."

"You mean a woman that fine actually deigned to speak to a guy like you?"

"A few words. I'm thinking there'll be more if I board a horse at her place."

"Wait. Hold it. What horse?"

The phone at his elbow rang, the first line lit up bright red. He grabbed the receiver, since Frank was taking his last bite of the cookies.

"Hello, Sheriff," said the sweetest voice ever.

"Kendra." Did he sound way too unprofessional or what? He cleared his throat and tried to sound more dignified. "What can I do for you on this fine morning?"

"I've got some good news for you."

"I like the sound of that. Frank and I polished off the last of your cookies, crumbs and all. Thank you. Haven't had better cookies."

"I'm glad you liked them."

Was it his imagination, or did she sound glad to talk to him?

"I may have found the perfect horse for you."

"Worked on that mighty fast, did you?"

"That's my job. I put out a few feelers, and guess what? I just got off the phone with a former client. I taught his kids to ride, and they're a very fine family of horse lovers. They have a gelding they're interested in selling, but only to someone who will be good to him. He's a registered quarter horse, but they are willing to budge on the price quite a bit. They'd rather he went to a good home."

Nerves coiled in the pit of his stomach. This was a big step. He was ready for it, but… "I don't want to make a mistake. Is he a good horse?"

"I trained him."

That said something. "Would *you* buy him, if you were me?"

"Absolutely. Warrior is a good-hearted animal. Plus, he's trained for the backwoods. The father and son are outdoorsmen, like yourself. The son's going off to college, and they don't want to sell, but they don't want the horse to be lonely, either. Would you like to look at him?"

"Would you come with me?"

"Sure. Let me check my schedule." He could hear Kendra flicking through her paperwork, all business. "I could do it this evening."

"So can I. Want me to ride out and pick you up?"
A man could always hope.

"Oh, no, that's going well out of your way."

"You're going out of yours to help me. The least I can do is provide the transportation."

"Don't worry about it. I do this all the time."

"As long as you're sure."

"Absolutely." Kendra couldn't believe what a nice guy Cameron was. She thought about what her sister had said. *The kind of man that stands tall and loves deep.*

Michelle was happily married. Maybe she knew the measure of a man when she looked at him. Kendra couldn't argue that Michelle was right.

Only the Lord knew how protective he'd been to her the night her life was in danger. How tall he'd stood. How strong.

How kind he'd been in the face of devastation and broken faith.

But if she ever trusted a man again, it would not be one who carried a gun on his hip. Not a man who stood strong against violence and won. The constant reminder of what she'd endured would just be too painful.

She squeezed her eyes shut, forcing away the image of Cameron on that cold, rainy October night taking Jerrod down. Fear took hold of her stomach.

Don't remember.

She cleared her throat. Business. That's what she had to focus on. And the fact that the Lord would not have led Cameron across her path once more if there wasn't a greater purpose. She'd received the sheriff's help; it was her chance to help him in return.

It felt right. Maybe it would help her find a way to forget and forgive. To bury that horrible time forever.

She forced cheer into her voice. "Do you know the Thornton's ranch? I'll meet you there at seven?"

"I'll be there. How do we do this? Do I need to bring my checkbook or anything?"

"You can, but you don't have to make a decision today. It's good to meet the horse and see if your personalities mesh, if he's what you want in a friend. A lot of folks look at a dozen or more horses before they find the right one."

"How do you know when you do?"

"You just *know*. You feel it in your heart. Do you know what I mean?"

Boy, did he. He had to wonder what he was feeling inside at this moment.

As he said goodbye and replaced the phone in the cradle, he realized he wasn't alone in the office. Frank was sitting across the room at his desk, staring right at him, one eyebrow raised—whether in disdain or approval, it was hard to tell.

I get to look at a horse tonight. It was all he could do to hold back his excitement. It made him want to get up and do a happy dance right in the middle of the street, but he restrained himself.

He settled for a second cup of coffee instead. Life was looking up. For the first time in a long while, he was glad to be alive.

As she kicked up a cloud of dust behind her pickup, barreling down the country road to the Thornton ranch, it hit her. Should she be speeding when she knew a sheriff was around? Not that she was speeding badly, just pushing the needle a little over the legal limit. She was running late.

Better late than a lawbreaker. Or having to pay for a ticket. She eased her foot off the gas and not a moment too soon. There was a gray patrol cruiser. Was it Cameron?

No, she realized as she moved over on the narrow road to give the oncoming car plenty of room. It was the new deputy. He had his window down and saluted her as they both slowed.

"Going a little fast, weren't you?" Easygoing and polite, the deputy flashed a grin at her.

"Yeah." It hurt to admit it. "I'm late meeting your boss."

"It's awful generous of you to help him out like this. He seems to really want a horse."

Was it her imagination, or did the deputy seem sarcastic? Not mean sarcastic, but as if he knew something she didn't. Oh, wait, she knew what he thought. He thought she had a crush on Cameron, too.

Her face grew hot. Really! Bake cookies as a thank-you, as a good gesture, and look what happens. She was really starting to regret making those cookies.

It had been all her sisters could talk about last night, when they were *supposed* to be having a sisters night, talking about what really mattered. Not about her ridiculous, nonexistent *thing* for poor Cameron. He had enough on his plate grieving his wife and trying to get on with his life.

"Just doing my job." She shrugged, knowing it was a lame answer, but it was the truth.

"And I'm doing mine. Would you mind handing over your license and registration?"

"Not going to let me get away with it, are you?" Resigned, Kendra grabbed the registration from behind the visor and rummaged through her purse for her ID. She handed it through the window. "I couldn't have been going more than three, four miles over the limit. I know, because I was afraid Cameron was going to catch me."

Frank studied her license. "You got a birthday coming up."

"In a few weeks."

"Well, I suppose it would only be decent of me, since I'm that kind of guy, to let this slide once." Was that a hint of trouble sparkling in Frank's eyes, as he held out her license?

"You are? Oh, that's great. Thank you."

"Wait. You didn't let me finish. You know how it goes. I do something for you, you do something for me. Chocolate-chip cookies. Lots of them." He saluted her as he drove away.

More cookies? She was going to have to bake more cookies? She would rather have had the ticket!

Cameron was waiting for her in his SUV when she pulled up. There was no way she was going to explain why she was late. She'd just drop the cookies off sometime when he was out on patrol. It couldn't be too hard to figure out, since he parked along the curb whenever he was in the office, right?

"I was beginning to think you'd stood me up for a better-looking guy." He adjusted his Stetson. "Have any trouble?"

"I'm always into trouble, you must know that by now."

"Yeah, I pegged you for trouble the day I moved back to this town. Riding horses. Building your own business. Sad you have no sense of responsibility."

"You're in a good mood. You're excited about this. You should be. Getting your first horse will bring about a wonderful change in your life. I promise you."

"I'll hold you to that." He looked changed from the quiet, stoic officer she'd seen around town for years.

This evening, as the sun sank low in the sky, he seemed more alive.

This was what she loved. Walking along a newly painted fence line with the scent of horse on the breeze. Seeing three saddle horses, two geldings and a mare she trained, grazing in the shade near the creek. The crunch of gravel beneath her riding boots. The anticipation of seeing Warrior again, and the Thorntons, who were good people.

"Sure is nice of you going to all this trouble for me."

"Stop thanking me. I love horses, and I hope you will, too."

"Been looking forward to this all day." He slowed to match his pace with hers. "The owners are negotiable?"

"I spoke to them again just before I left." She gestured toward the stable, bypassing the house, as if she'd been here many times before. "Mr. Thornton is more concerned with their horse finding a good home rather than what money they get for him. There he is. The black one in the paddock."

"The all-black one?" He looked like a show horse, all gleam and polish and fine bold lines. Cam might know next to nothing about horses, but he could see this was a quality animal. "That one looks too fancy for what I need."

"He's a trained trail horse, for all terrain and all seasons. He can pack, hunt, jump, lead and rope."

"Sounds like what I'm looking for. Hi, fella." He held out his palm.

The big animal studied him with intelligent eyes. He was huge, the biggest horse Cam had seen yet. The animal's big velvet nostrils flared as the gelding sniffed his hand, then nickered low in his throat.

Could he handle him? Cam wondered.

As if in answer, the horse nosed him. A spark of

affection flashed to life in Cam's chest, like a flint striking kindling. What a fine horse he was.

"Hi there, Evan!" Kendra waved in a rider trotting into sight from the hillside trails. "Your horse is lookin' good."

"The work you did with her sure helped her gait. Hi, Cameron." Evan swung down from the saddle.

"Howdy." He knew Evan well enough, he'd been years older in school. He was without a wife these days. Is that why Cameron felt protective? Or was it jealous?

That realization made him uneasy. Jealous? He didn't like to think he could let that undesirable emotion into his heart. But he couldn't deny a certain fierce urge to make sure Evan kept his distance from Kendra.

Kendra didn't seem to notice as she stroked her sensitive fingertips down Warrior's neck and spoke to Evan Thornton as if they were old friends. "Is Kevin glad to be heading off to his second year of college?"

Evan's affirmative answer sounded somewhere in the distance. All Cameron saw was Kendra. The world around him had disappeared; there was only her. The soft spring scent of flowers, the feel of her, as if it wasn't just his heart reacting, but his soul was aware of hers.

How was it he could feel her spirit? Strange, the power of it. He didn't understand what was happening. Only that he'd never seen such beauty in his life—and he wasn't referring to the glitzy, primp-in-front-of-the-mirror kind. Hers was a beauty that lasted. It shone from the inside and made the lovely woman she was all the more breathtaking.

Dressed in a plain gray T-shirt, ordinary faded jeans and scuffed riding boots, she was extraordinary. His chest ached with the wonder of it.

"He likes you." Kendra smiled and it was like the first day of spring after a long and bleak winter. "Evan, can we take Warrior for a ride?"

"Sure thing. His saddle's in the tack room in the barn. Want me to do the honors?"

"I can handle it. What do you think, Cameron?"

The poor man looked love struck. "I'd like to, but the truth is, I think he's way too fine for the likes of me."

"I think he's perfect for you." Who would have thought that the strong and practical town sheriff would fall head over heels for a horse? She couldn't be happier for him. "You like the mountains, and he does, too."

The gelding nudged him, nearly knocking him off his feet. "Whoa, fella. Take it easy on me."

"See? He feels the same. Maybe he can sense you two are kindred spirits. He's been lonely for the whole year Evan's son has been away at college. He wants someone who likes to ride high up into the back-country and camp and fish and hunt."

"I can't ride worth squat. You know I just sat on that horse of yours, Palouse. I imagine Warrior is used to a skilled rider. Someone who knows how to handle him.''

.''So, you'll take lessons. I'll teach you to ride him. You can stop off in the evenings after work to spend time with him. Get to know him. Develop a bond and trust between you.''

Exactly. If God answers prayers and can look straight into a man's heart to see the goodness through all the bad, then the Lord would see how much he wanted this.

The Lord might see, too, how Cameron was thinking about more than the horse.

''You've got a deal, Kendra McKaslin. You teach me to ride him, and I'll buy him.''

''Oh, what a lucky horse you are, Warrior.'' Kendra shone with all the beauty of a summer's sunset.

Words died in his throat. No, he was the lucky one. Cameron said nothing more. He didn't have to. He felt as light as air, as Kendra smiled, just for him, like a gift from above.

Chapter Seven

Okay, here goes nothing. Kendra clutched the paper plate stacked high with cookies and marched straight to the front door. A banner advertising the upcoming Harvest Days festival flapped overhead as she hurried past the antique shop and into the sheriff's air-conditioned office.

"You remembered." Frank rose from behind his paper-piled desk, but he looked uncomfortable instead of glad to see more cookies. "Cam isn't in. He stepped out for a few minutes. Ran out to grab us both a couple drinks from your sister's coffee shop."

"Too bad there isn't a doughnut shop in town." Kendra quipped so she didn't have to comment on Cameron's being absent, because she'd timed it that way. She'd spotted his cruiser pulling away from the curb from the Feed and Grain store, where she was putting in her monthly order.

But if he went to the coffee shop, that was like four blocks away. In this heat, it made sense he would drive, but that meant it was a short trip. He'd be back any second!

"Hope this fulfills the requirement, Deputy." She slipped the covered plate on the edge of his desk. "Thanks again for looking past my indiscretion. I have been very careful with my speed every since."

"I'm glad to hear it. Mmm." He bit into a cookie like a hungry kid.

She took advantage of his chewing to head straight for the door. "Have a great afternoon!" she called, and she was free. Safely on the sidewalk, escaping before Cameron—

"Where's the fire?" a friendly baritone rumbled as two big hands caught her elbows, stopping her before she ran full speed into him.

Cameron. Her heart stopped. Already he'd released her, but the imprint of his fingers banding her arms remained. Her mouth opened, but she couldn't think of anything to say.

"Hey, did Evan Thornton get a hold of you? He said he'd trailer my new horse over to your place sometime late this afternoon. I figured I'd pop on over to your place to see him."

There was something wrong with her mind. It wasn't working right. It was as if her neurotransmitters had forgotten how to fire. All she could do was stare up at the man towering over her, looking dashing in the well-fitted uniform.

"I'm taking your advice. I'm going to go slow, spend time with Warrior. Let him see I'm the best friend he's ever gonna have."

"F-fine." There, at least her tongue was starting to work, although she sounded lame and half-dazed.

Had he always had such an amazing smile? Kendra couldn't seem to remember but her feet were carrying her down the sidewalk. Cameron watched after her, as if he were making sure she wasn't likely to plow into someone else head-on.

"I'll see you tonight, then," he called the length of the sidewalk. "Is there anytime you consider too late to stay? You must close up shop sometime."

"Uh, until dark?"

She didn't sound too sure of her answer. Cameron figured not too many folks stayed out with their horses late into the evening. Well, wasn't that nice? He was interested in her. He'd be able to spend more time with her.

A hard band of fear tightened around his chest. Was that really a good idea? Was he ready to start caring about another woman? He didn't know if he could ever risk his heart again. He wouldn't trade a second of his time with Debra. He'd loved her deeply. Losing her had been the toughest thing that ever happened to him. He couldn't go through that again.

"Where's the iced tea?" Frank asked from behind his computer monitor.

"Closed. They're cutting back hours, I guess."

"I'd be mad, but guess what? I wrangled more

cookies out of your girlfriend.'' With a sly grin, Frank bit into a chocolate cookie.

"She's not my girlfriend.'' Cam helped himself. The plate was stacked high—had to be two-dozen cookies. "Way to go. How did you finagle this?''

"I was just out patrolling. Doing my job like a good deputy. I couldn't help it that she was going twenty-six in a twenty-five zone. I *had* to reprimand her.''

"You had no choice.''

"Exactly. Know what else I found out? Her birth date. It's coming up, too. Thought you might want to know.''

"Why? I'm not exactly a member of her inner circle.''

"But my guess is that you might want an invitation to the party. If you can't admit it to yourself yet, then fine. Denial is as good of a way to cope as any.'' Frank hit a key and the shared printer came to life, spitting and sputtering in the corner.

"I thought you didn't approve of her.''

"It's not my call. But admit it. You like the woman.'' He scribbled something on a memo pad.

"Sure, I like her. Who doesn't like her?'' She was friendly and beautiful and helpful. What wasn't to like?

Cam knew perfectly well that wasn't the kind of *like* Frank was talking about. He meant romantic interest. That was exactly what Cam was wondering, too.

* * *

It hadn't been the best day. Kendra left the cordless phone on the desk. It *looked* as though she had enough of a crew to cut hay, although she couldn't be sure.

She wasn't offering top dollar—she was meeting a good field wage, but she didn't have the capital right now to compete with her neighbors for the limited amount of teenagers and part-time field-workers in the valley.

She couldn't blame the workers for wanting to make the most pay they could, but if she heard one more, "I'll come in the morning if Mr. Brisbane's crew is already full," she was going to, well, do the entire haying herself.

"You look beat," Colleen commented from where she was upending a grain bucket into a stall trough. "Did you need help making any calls? I don't mind playing the tough guy."

"Thanks, I may take you up on that tomorrow. I have ten delinquent accounts and they keep avoiding me. I've left messages, I keep trying to hunt them down in the arena. Nothing." Kendra didn't add that she could really use that money. Things were tight—but then, they were always tight. Just a part of being an upstart business, that was all.

"If you want to show me the list, I can help you hunt them down in person." Colleen swiped the sweat from her forehead.

Colleen was a hard worker, and one day she wanted to open a stable of her own. It would be good to teach her more of the business side of things. "Meet me in my office first thing tomorrow."

"Awesome." Colleen flashed a grateful smile before refilling the ten-gallon bucket. "Oh, I forgot. The sheriff's new horse came in while you were out in the fields. I got Warrior settled in a nice corner box stall like you asked."

"You are wonderful, Colleen. Thanks." Kendra took a step, saw Trisha Corey, fresh off work, head down the aisle toward her horse's stall. Seeing the woman reminded her that Cameron would be coming by soon, as he'd promised. "Can you do me a favor?"

"Name it."

"Could you show the sheriff to his horse when he gets here? Answer his·questions, that kind of thing? I haven't really gone over a lot of things with him yet." Oh, and the contract. She had to get his contract printed out.

Her stomach rumbled. She had skipped lunch again. Maybe she'd print off the paperwork while she cooked something quick to eat. Oh, and she had to balance the checkbook so she knew if she could make a payment to the feed store.

She mentally added that to her list as she swept down the main aisle toward the back exit. The long diaphanous rays of the evening sun streamed through the double doors like a path at her feet.

She noticed Cameron's dark blue SUV ambling down her graveled driveway. True to his word, he'd come to spend time with his horse.

It was the hand of Providence that brought the right horse in his direction, and she was glad for him. As she followed the rail paddock toward her little cottage tucked on the rising knoll of the property, she had a perfect view as he parked, climbed out, adjusted his Stetson and glanced her way. His hand shot up in the air in a manly wave.

For one fleeting second, a tide of joy lifted her up. Happiness? No, she *couldn't* be happy to see him. What sense did that make? She was glad he'd come for his horse's sake. That was all.

She stopped to check the roses in her backyard garden, grabbed the shears and snipped off a few fragrant yellow blossoms on her way in. Her cat was a huge marmalade lump on the couch cushion in front of the air conditioner. He opened one eye a slit, appraised her mildly, then let his eye droop.

"Good to see you, too, handsome. Don't get up or anything." She snagged a bud vase from the shelf over the refrigerator and filled it with lukewarm water. She heard the thud as he jumped down from his perch.

He wove his way around her ankles, mewing pointedly.

"I know. I'm sorry. I'm late." Where did she put the can opener? "You know what I need? Two can openers, so when I lose one, I can still open—"

She felt a change in the air, like a charge of anticipation before a thunderstorm. It trickled across her skin like a temperate breeze. It filled her senses like the sharp, heavy smell of ozone that accompanied thunder.

Cameron. She *felt* him. She saw him without turning around, striding with that easy gait of his, relaxed because he'd changed out of his uniform and was wearing those worn-comfortable jeans and a plain T-shirt that made him look like a hero out of a western.

Every cell of her being focused on the tap of boots against the wooden porch.

"Do you always do that?" His baritone shivered over her.

"Do what?" She couldn't think again. "Lose my can opener?"

"Talk to your cat. As fine as he is, he can't talk back."

"No, but he makes faces like a teenager, so I figure there has to be some cognitive function behind the sneer. See? He lifted his lip at me."

"I've never had a cat. Call me a dog person. Well, a horse person now." He was wearing a grin that showed off two dimples to perfection.

She placed the vase and delicate roses on the breakfast bar, where she intended to eat her supper, whatever it might be. But first, she'd deal with Cameron. "Have you seen Warrior yet?"

"Gave him a pat on the way by. The gal that works for you, Colleen, was real helpful, but I told her I needed to see you."

She hadn't realized he was holding one hand behind

his back until he produced a small present, wrapped in black-and-gray-striped paper with a bow taped to the center. "A gift? But why?"

"To thank you. You went out of your way for me, helped me, and I sure appreciated it." He set the offering on the edge of her kitchen table.

What a nice, thoughtful man he is. Clearly, wrapped in the plain paper, it was nothing romantic or inappropriate. And how could she say no? "I truly don't need a gift."

"It's good manners. Besides, after baking us another round of cookies, I figure it's a fair trade. Butter and sugar costs money." He winked, so she knew he was using humor to lower her defenses, to make it all right. "Go ahead and open it."

She eyed him suspiciously for a moment, and panic knotted behind her sternum. A gift. That wasn't appropriate at all, was it? Should she give it back? "This is too much."

"You don't know how much I was sweatin' all this stuff. What horse? What kind of horse? Would I pay too much? Or get a lemon? Would I even like riding? It's been bugging me for months, and you come along and make it so easy. Thank you."

The corners of her soft mouth quirked as she plucked the bow off the package. It was all he could do to stand still while she pulled carefully at the layer of wrapping tape he'd used on both ends.

"This package is hard to break into." She studied

him through her thick lashes as she reached into a drawer and pulled out a small pair of sharp scissors.

He knew what she was doing. She was watching for any hint of romantic intentions. That's why he'd used black paper, which was about as far away from romantic paper as a guy could get, he figured. And why he purposefully tried to act indifferent, even if his pulse was thudding so hard in his chest he swore she could see it against his shirt. All this was telling him Frank might be right. He might *like* Kendra. More than he wanted to admit.

"Oh, Cameron. Thank you." The loose strands of gold that had escaped her ponytail throughout her long day's work framed her face in soft waves. True pleasure drew color into her cheeks. Her eyes sparkled as she pulled the DVD case from the wrapping paper. It was one of her favorite westerns.

"Do you have it already?"

"No. I've been renting instead of working on my movie collection." She gestured to the other side of the room where a small TV sat on what looked like a newly varnished antique trunk. On top of it sat an economy-model DVD player and a set of rabbit ears.

"A collection, huh? That sounds impressive."

"Yeah, doesn't it?" She crossed in front of a small coffee table and a covered, overstuffed couch to set the DVD case next to the TV. "Now I have, wow, one movie. It's a *very* selective collection."

"You have good taste." He didn't have to wonder to see how tight Kendra's budget had to be. She'd made those curtains herself, he figured, since his Deb had sewn and he recognized the touches no discount-store-bought item could provide.

The furniture was all secondhand and probably older than either one of them, but it was dusted and polished, refinished and cozy. The cottage was small and feminine—there were ruffles and lace, not a lot of it, but even a small amount was too much for a tough guy like him. It made the back of his neck itch.

He felt like a bull penned in a field of daisies in this small feminine home next to this petite, feminine woman. For all the hard physical labor she must have to do to earn her living, she was really a wisp of a thing, all long limbs and quiet elegance.

Tenderness flickered to life in his chest and glowed like a candle's soft radiance. *Lord, are you trying to tell me something?* "I'd best let you get to your supper. What are you making?"

"I'm clueless. I haven't browsed through my cupboards yet."

"I don't imagine you have a lot of time for cooking."

"I manage, since the other option is starving to death."

"It's hard to cook for just one person. If I whip up something like lasagna on the weekend, then I wind up eating it all week."

"You could freeze portions in those little freezer bags. The kind that lock out freezer burn. That's what

I do. Except then I run out of time to cook or shop, especially this time of year.''

She yanked open the secondhand appliance—it had to be a good thirty years old, since it was the shade of yellow popular in the seventies. ''See? That's what I do with my hamburger. Make them ahead and freeze them.''

''That's a smart idea. I ought to try that.'' He would—except that he wound up making a sandwich more often than not. He'd never gotten used to the quiet of the kitchen in the evening. He and Deb always used to cook together. ''Well, I guess I'll head back to the stable.''

''Want to stay? I have extra patties I could defrost.'' Now why did she ask that?

Because it made the loneliness that lined his face vanish. ''They wouldn't be too much trouble?''

''Not if you want to start the barbecue for me.'' After all, his gift had her feeling guilty.

''I'm a pro when it comes to barbecuing.'' There was no mistaking the ridge of muscle that flexed and stretched his white T-shirt. No mistaking the power of the gun holstered at his hip. ''Matches?''

''In the top drawer closest to you.''

The sheriff's step was light, his grin cheerful. She liked him this way—steady and as dependable as the Bridger Mountains, but buoyant, too. Maybe it was because he was stepping out of the last stages of his grief.

Her door squeaked shut. A sharp, punctuated

"Meow!" had her looking down at the cat still glaring with disapproval.

"Be nice," she told him with a laugh. "He's not staying. He's just passing through."

Pounce did not seem reassured, even after she forked his favorite salmon cat food into his food dish and broke it up into small chunks for him.

She'd never ever had a man in her house before, aside from her dad and brothers-in-law. Cameron's presence was tangible, although he was on the deck out of sight. She felt the masculine power of his being. It shrank the already too small kitchen, it filled her tiny house and made her feel vulnerable.

The grill's lid squeaked as he lifted it. She heard the strike of a match, smelled the flare of sulfur and the burn of residue from the grill. The scrape as he cleaned the metal rack. The *clink* of the lid lowering into place.

He was a big man. He filled the door frame as he strolled inside, replaced the box of matches and planted his hands on the edge of the counter. "Anything else you need done?"

"Nope." She hit a button and the microwave began humming. She'd acted on impulse. When was acting on impulse the *best* idea? Never!

"Better make use of me while I'm here. I'm pretty good at making a salad."

"Define salad for me. My experience with men is that they avoid vegetables as if they're poison."

"Not true. Throw bacon on it, and I'll eat it. Even a heap of lettuce leaves."

"Just what I thought. I'm not about to trust you with the single most important part of the meal."

"The meat?"

She rolled her eyes. "Lettuce from my garden. Fresh carrots straight from the garden. I'm going out to pick a tomato."

"I can do it."

"I'm sure you can." She had images of her father bumbling around her mom's garden before he was banned for life.

"You don't think I know what I'm doing?"

"What man does?" In a flash, she'd taken a plastic bag from the second drawer and was out the door. "Do you have to follow me?"

"I've got to prove myself. I can't have you thinking I'm a failure when it comes to picking vegetables. My reputation is at stake. I've got the election to think about."

"Aren't you running uncontested?"

"Sure, but there's always the write-in option. I can't have a surprise last-minute candidate stealing my job." He knelt down beside her in the soft earth. "How many carrots do you need?"

"Sixty. Maybe seventy." She brushed away the loose dirt from a carrot's base, the feathery leaves tickling her forearm as she grasped and pulled.

He was scowling at her. "I'm going to pretend I didn't hear that." He twisted a plump red tomato off its rambling vine. "Is it just me, or do you treat all your boarders like this?"

"Boarders aren't allowed in my yard."

"Guess I'm just special."

"Nope. I haven't given you the printout with all the rules on it yet."

"I'm breaking some kind of law being up here?"

She shook loose dirt off the carrot and plunked it into the sack. "I suppose there's exceptions to every rule, Officer, but as you know, that comes with a price. I guess you owe *me* a plate of cookies."

"You play tough but fair."

"I'm only kidding. You don't owe me any cookies. My house and yard are off-limits. I'm hardly ever here. I'm almost always down at the stable or riding most of the day, but when I'm here I just want a few quiet minutes."

"I know how that is, since I'm always on call." He added a tomato to her bag. "It's not so bad. Frank and I split weekend duties. You know, patrolling the roads, keeping an eye out for mischief, making sure no one's driving drunk, as far as we can tell."

"I never gave it much thought." She plucked a fat, sweet cuke from the vine and, taking the bag with her, rose to check the tassels on the corn. "You must have to give up a lot of evenings."

"It's an honor, serving the people of this fine town." He didn't know how else to say it. It sounded hokey, and he was embarrassed, but he was proud, too. Proud of the difference he made in people's lives every day.

"Even if it's just lending a hand with a trailer tire, or making sure a mother with two little kids isn't stuck in bad weather when her car breaks down. There isn't a lot of crime in these parts, but I'm there if anyone needs me."

Would Kendra understand? She had to know, more than most, what he was prepared to do to serve and protect. He dug his thumb into gold tassels and smiled at the bright yellow husks beneath. "How many do you want?"

"You pick what you can eat."

"Got any real butter to go along with this? I can eat a lot."

"Real butter. I just might let you use the salt and pepper, too."

"Pepper? Uh." He winked at her as he snapped off two ears of corn, followed by two more. "How many are you picking? Five, no, six. You can eat that much corn? A little skinny thing like you?"

"Half of this is for Colleen. I'm going to give her a jingle and ask her to join us."

"Don't trust me enough to be alone with me, is that it?" His heart drummed as if he'd run his usual seven daily miles all uphill. He was teasing, but he wasn't.

Something crossed over Kendra's face, a shade of emotion that made her eyes darken. "We're not alone, Officer."

As if in answer, her big plump cat curled around

his ankles. A horse's nicker lifted on the wind. There, looking at him with a stare of unveiled assessment were two horses, the ones he recognized from the stable that one day, and the pretty golden mare she'd ridden on the trail.

She kept her animals in the paddock closest to her house, did she? They were watching his every move with great interest as he trailed Kendra over to the board fence.

"I'll leave you to do this. Just toss the husks over the fence and let them duke it out." Kendra rolled the corn ears gently to the ground. "I'll go start the salad, check the meat and give Colleen a call."

"Sure thing." Here he'd been hoping this would be a supper for two. The least Kendra could do was to stay and husk the corn with him, so he could watch her sparkle in the sun and try to charm a few more smiles out of her.

She tapped away down the flagstone path, wound through the pleasant tangle of bright roses flowering every which way and color, then disappeared into the house.

Without her, it seemed as if the daylight had dimmed. He waited for a glimpse of her while he husked corn. The horses jockeyed closer, stretching their necks eagerly over the top rail.

He caught sight of Kendra at her kitchen window, washing vegetables while she chatted with the phone tucked between her shoulder and her cheek.

Disappointed wasn't the word he would use to describe the rake of pain in his heart. It was much worse.

Night wrung the last of twilight from the sky. The last traces of magenta and purple brushed the underbellies of nimbus clouds and then retreated into darkness.

Kendra tapped a few numbers on the keyboard and double-checked them on the screen to the numbers scribbled in her green columned ledger. She was halfway through her accounts receivable posting, and her eyelids kept drooping.

A yawn nearly split her in two. She hit Save and left the cursor blinking. Steam from her cup of vanilla red tea invited her to take another sweet, spicy sip. Over the top of the rim she could see the twin beams of headlights pulling out of the gravel parking area down below.

Colleen's pickup, it looked like, ambled a few yards and then hesitated. Was a horse out? Kendra wondered and just as quickly realized a SUV's dome light flashed on. She recognized the faint profile—Cameron.

Colleen and Cameron were talking. During supper at her small table, Cameron had regaled them with funny tales about his last fishing expedition and the last time he'd been shopping in the mall, how he got lost in a department store he couldn't get out of. He'd had them laughing too hard to eat.

Had he been trying to charm Colleen? Maybe so. Kendra took another sip and watched as the pickup rolled ahead, lumbering down the roll and bends of the driveway and out of sight.

Cameron's dome light died. The lights flared on and he drove away into the darkness.

Why did it seem as if something were tugging at her soul? She couldn't describe the sensation, her protective shields were up and fully functional so she couldn't feel what was behind those steel walls.

Cameron was a widower. Colleen was alone, too. Maybe it was Providence that had a hand in their coming together. Cameron would be coming often to visit his horse, to take lessons and to ride the trails when he was more accomplished.

Maybe she could make sure that Cameron wound up in Colleen's classes. Who knew where that would lead? Maybe the two of them would find they had a lot in common. Maybe they'd begin dating. Fall in love.

Wouldn't that be great for them? Why did that make her ache, when she'd vowed not to feel anything at all?

The hum of the computer fan in its casing sounded noisy. As loud as the window unit in the other room. She set her cup onto the ceramic coaster with a clink that sounded as jarring as a gunshot.

The quiet echoed around her. The emptiness inside her echoed, too. She was tired, that was all. Some nights the solitary life she'd chosen weighed on her heavily.

But it was a safe life, she reminded herself as she

gathered the daily checks together, stamped the back of them and tucked them into an envelope for tomorrow's deposit.

Shadows moved in the gathering darkness outside. Her horses came to check on her before bedtime, crowding together to try to get a look at her through the window. Three horses and the shorter, limping gait of her old pony. Their silhouettes pushed at the rail fence. A sharp neigh was a welcoming sound in the stillness.

"I'm coming, Honeybear." She left her tea and computer, squeezed along the narrow space between her bed and the wall, for the room was small, to the doorway.

Pounce opened his eyes a slit to follow her progress through the living room to the back door. She grabbed a handful of candies on the way out, the heat of the summer's evening a shock on her skin as she loped out to meet her best friends.

Her sweet gray-and-white pony, the one she'd learned to ride on, as had all of her sisters, crowded the fence. They'd always had a close bond. She gave him a peppermint first, the poor old guy, and he nudged her hand in affectionate thanks.

Jingles snorted, shaking her head as if she was in command, demanding a candy next.

"Oh, you think you're all that, don't you?" The quarter horse knew she was, and Kendra wasn't going to argue with her. She doled out the candy, ran her fingers through Jingles's mane and through Honey-bear's forelock before giving Sprite the last mint.

Deer were daring to make their way through the field grasses, cautiously moving with the darkness. The sounds of night coming—the hoot of an owl, the sharp, high cry of a distant coyote, the whoosh of a horse exhaling as it settled down in its stall for the night drifted on the warm, temperate breezes, buoying her spirits.

This was her life. It wasn't the one she'd always thought she would have. She could almost hear the echoes of that life—the warm rumble of a good man's voice in the kitchen behind her, the distant laughter of happy children—but then the memories weighed down her heart.

Her life was a good one, and she was thankful for the peace of the evening. Maybe she'd head down to the barn and check on Willow. Make sure everything was settled for the night.

Night chased the last of the shadows from the earth. Kendra climbed through the fence, greeting her friends, and they accompanied her through the darkness, following the worn dirt path by feel and by memory. She didn't mind the coming night or the darkness surrounding her, for it made the stars shine all the brighter.

Chapter Eight

Cameron's evenings fell into a rhythm. After his workday was done, and barring any emergencies or calls, he'd head home for a quick bite and a faster shower before driving all the way out to Kendra's ranch.

Once on his trip out, he caught sight of her in the seat of the cutter, riding the ten-year-old machine in the golden fields that paralleled her mile-long driveway. He waved, but she couldn't have seen him with the sun's glare in her eyes.

When he'd asked the helpful Colleen if Kendra was avoiding him or something, she'd only said it was a busy time of year, with haying the hundred acres—of her own hay fields plus those she leased every summer.

Sure, he could see that. But did she work all the time? He tried dropping by to slip Warrior a treat early before he started his morning patrols, but Kendra was already in the fields, or so the teenager cleaning stalls told him.

The one evening he did spot her, it was late and she was out in the far field, nothing more than a willowy slip in the distance. She stood still with a hand outstretched to a magnificent red horse who looked ready to charge her instead of accept whatever treat she held flat on her palm.

After he'd said hello to Warrior—the horse had been awful glad to see him—he bided his time figuring Kendra would have to come in when the night wrung the twilight from the sky. But no, she'd untethered her golden horse from the fence and rode off bareback into the hills.

He waited another hour, long after the last employee had finished with her chores. No Kendra. He'd given up, wearing his loneliness like a too big coat on a hot day.

He was forced to deal with Colleen, Kendra's second in command, when it came to decisions about Warrior's care. He signed a contract and wrote a check to McKaslin's Riding Stable and studied the class schedule. A new session of beginners' lessons started soon and it was something to consider. Colleen offered him private lessons, since the group lessons were mostly little girls on their first horses or ponies.

When he asked when Kendra would be available to give private lessons, he was flat-out stonewalled.

"Oh, not until sometime after haying season. It's a

busy time of year, and you don't want to put off learning to ride Warrior, right? These are the last sessions
before school starts.''

Even thinking about it now, in the quiet of his patrol
car, annoyed him. He knew Kendra was busy, but
twice he'd spotted her in the stable when he'd pulled
into the driveway. By the time he'd parked, she was
gone. He'd respected her rules and hadn't ventured up
to knock on her back door again. He knew she wasn't
there anyway.

When he'd checked the schedule, Kendra was listed
as the teacher for several advanced classes, things like
barrel racing and Western show. There was one beginners' class she offered two afternoons a week.

Avoiding him? Yep. He'd wager money on it and
he wasn't a betting man. Did she feel the same way
he did? That there was an attraction between them?
Something with potential, and maybe she wasn't interested in pursuing it?

Don't read too much into that, man. She's busy
running her business. He didn't know if he wanted to
risk his heart again and go through the pain of loving
in a world with no guarantees. And yet the time with
Debra had been worth all the pain and more.

He wasn't a waiting man. Not anymore. Life was a
precious gift and he couldn't waste it, walking through
life, filling his days with loneliness. Did that mean he
was ready to love again? Maybe he ought to find out.

He'd thought maybe Saturday would be a good day,
and even traded the workday with Frank. But there

had been a sort of competition and show put on by Kendra and her employees.

Every time he saw her, she was judging a string of nervous-looking kids dressed in tooled Western wear perched atop glistening horses being put through paces and moves and inspections.

Maybe he'd sit with the rest of the spectators on the risers on the far side of the covered arena where it was shaded. He even deposited two quarters for a soda into a vending machine near the stands. The bubbling cola slid down his throat like ice, cooling him on what had to be the hottest day of the year.

Kendra was handing out ribbons for the winning riders. He noticed she had ribbons for every one of the grade-school-age kids.

Cam took his time circling around; the stable yard was jam-packed today.

He had all day off, thanks to his deal with Frank. His pager was off, his gun was locked in the closet at home and he was a free man. Free to wait Kendra out, even if it took until midnight to get her alone.

The tinder-dry grasses crackled beneath his boots as he headed for the shade. He noticed a cigarette butt someone had left smoldering behind the seating, despite the No Smoking At Any Time signs posted, and crushed it with his heel.

"Hi, Cameron," Cheryl Pittman called out.

They'd gone to school together. She'd married, had kids and put her minivan in a ditch last year when the winter winds had frozen the rain on the road. He'd driven her and her kids home that day.

He nodded a polite greeting. "Howdy, Cheryl. Is your oldest competing in the show today?"

"She sure is! Caitlin's already won two blue ribbons. It sure is a nice setup Kendra has here, don't you think? Great for the kids. I hear you bought yourself that fine hunter the Thorntons had up for sale."

"Guilty. Hope you have a good day, Cheryl." He tipped his hat, moving on, studying the families that had gathered to watch their kids compete.

It didn't take much to see how his future *could* be with Kendra. Kendra's life was her family and her horses, anyone with an eye could see that.

Sundays would be enjoyed with her family, the sisters taking turns hosting the meal and spending the evening together.

The rest of the weekends and evenings would be spent in the stable. He had no problem with that, once he figured out how to be halfway as good a horseman so that he could keep up with her.

He watched a pair of little girls, probably second- or third-graders, ride by on their horses, giggling and looking as wholesome and as happy as children ought to be.

This would be a great place to raise kids. The thought stuck with him as he climbed the bleachers, nodded hello to everyone who said hi. He'd grown up in this town. Add that to being the local law, and he knew just about everyone.

He found a lonely stretch of bench and settled down to keep an eye on Miss McKaslin.

All his senses were filled by the slender woman looking at home in a sleeveless cotton top, faded jeans and black leather boots. Her hair was pulled back into a soft ponytail that swung with her easy, graceful stride.

Cameron couldn't help noticing the hard ridge of her shoulder blades edging the back of her shirt and the knob of bone at the curve of her elbow. She was spare, not a lot to her for all her strength and her self-sufficiency.

Tenderness warmed the center of his chest thinking about how fragile she looked, those fine bones of hers, the lean cords of muscles in her forearms as she unlatched a gate with her narrow, agile fingers.

The tenderness inside him grew. Like the burst of light, suddenly so bright at dawn as the sun broke boldly over the mountain range, that's what it was like. One moment he was sitting in shadows, and the next he was too blinded to see. He was overwhelmed by the intense desire to be the man who would love her for all the days to come. To keep her safe and cherished and happy.

He loved her. Just like that. Like gravity suddenly snaring a hunk of meteorite and yanking it through space.

"Sheriff?" It was one of the stable girls holding a cordless phone. "The, um, deputy's asking for you."

That could only mean one thing. An emergency. He

thanked the girl, took the phone and said goodbye to any chance of seeing Kendra—again.

The remnants of smoke hazed the evening sky as Kendra nosed Sprite off the main road through town. It was quiet, the businesses closed, the sidewalk empty, only a few cars parked in front of the few restaurants in town.

The black scorched earth next to the road was visible on this end of the street. Like an ugly scar, it marred the golden crisp fields on the far side of town and into the distance, smoldering. A local fire truck was pulled to the side of the road, the men probably looking for hot spots. The acrid scent lifted and fell with the breeze.

She reined her gelding down the closest alley and spied a familiar SUV idling in line at the drive-in's take-out window. Why was her first thought to turn around and head somewhere else? Wrong. Cameron was a client and an acquaintance.

Earlier today, she had felt his intense gaze when she'd been handing Brianna Pittman her second-place ribbon. She'd known the instant he'd stood from his place on the bleachers and left. She'd felt the change in the air.

There had been nearly fifty people in the stands watching the show. Maybe as many milling around. Why was she aware of the comings and goings of that one man?

She reined Sprite into place behind his vehicle. She

watched the line of his shoulders tense, as if he felt her presence, the way she felt his. Like autumn in the air. Like a change that couldn't be seen or measured, only felt.

He glanced in his rearview mirror. His side window lowered. "Is that legal?"

"What are you going to do, write me another ticket?"

"I could get a few more cookies out of you."

"What? You owe *me* cookies."

"I've been trying to pay you back, but you've been busy, I guess."

She shrugged. What was she going to say to that? She'd been trying to avoid him. She wasn't going to lie about it, but she didn't have to admit it, either. "Move ahead, Officer. You're holding up the line."

His vehicle eased ahead to the posted menu, and she listened to him order two bacon double cheeseburgers, onion rings and a huckleberry shake.

From her perch, she could see Cam's profile perfectly. The striking darkness of his short hair, which was very masculine on his square, chiseled face, and the hint of a day's growth on his jaw.

Why did her fingers itch to touch that stubble?

She couldn't deny the truth any longer. A truck pulled up behind her, brakes faintly squeaking as the sheriff moved on, cornering the building.

A teenager's cheerful voice crackled out of the thirty-year-old speaker. "Welcome to Misty's. Can I take your order?"

"A bacon double cheeseburger, onion rings and a huckleberry shake, please."

"Thank you! That will be three-seventy-three, please."

Kendra pulled the folded dollar bills she'd dug out of her purse and nudged Sprite ahead in line.

Two little girls rode up behind her.

"Hi, Kendra!" Caitlin Pittman said in unison with her best friend Tiffany Corey.

"Hi, you two." Kendra saw her past in a flash, how she used to ride to town with her sisters and best friends so long ago, to order double-dipped cones from the drive-through window.

It was a tradition in this town for little girls who had their own horses to ride.

The sheriff was reaching for his white paper bag of food. He pulled ahead, idling, while Kendra handed over her money in exchange for a bag and a big white cup of her own.

"Plan on riding home with that? Or eating here?"

"It's a mystery and I'm not telling you." She didn't mention they'd ordered the same meal. Lots of people liked bacon double cheeseburgers. Probably half of the town. "What happened? You were watching the show and then you weren't. Was it the fire west of town?"

"Grass fire. Some dolt must have tossed either his match or his cigarette butt out his window. We got it out before it took out any homes."

"I'm not surprised." Cameron was a powerful, capable man. He could do anything. "Stopping for a late supper?"

"Yep. I'm too beat from helping out the fire department to try to make something at home. I don't think I'll be heading out to see Warrior tonight."

"I'll give him a little time when I get home, on your behalf."

A little time. That's all he wanted. "You've got dinner and I've got dinner. We're both alone. We might as well eat alone together."

"I've got Sprite. I don't want to leave him outside while I go in."

"Then we can eat right here in the parking lot. How about it?"

"I'm only saying yes because I'm hoping you'll make good on your cookie promises."

"I've got something better than cookies." He pulled forward into a parking space before she could answer. Keep her guessing. Why not?

She swung down, graceful as a dream, and her big gelding followed her, hungrily trying to nip at the food bag. "I guess I can humor one of the men who gave up his Saturday to help put out a wildfire."

"Careful. You're making me sound noble."

"Right. We can't have that." She sat down beside him on the shady grass.

They sat nearly elbow-to-elbow, unpacking their food in silence. *Think of something brilliant, man. This is your chance to dazzle her.*

Then he noticed her order. It was the same as his.

See? It was a sign from above. "Did you get your hay in all right?"

"The barn is packed and ready for winter." She stole a crisp onion ring from the bag. "Every year it's getting harder to find field hands."

"I saw you out on the old cutter. Was it your dad's?"

"That's the great thing about having a farmer for a father. He gave me his old tractor, too."

"So, if you have your hay in, then you don't have any more reasons to avoid me. Do you? Unless you're having another competition next Saturday."

Heat swept up her neck and into her face. Had she been that obvious? She'd been hoping he hadn't noticed! "I *have* been busy." Trying to avoid you, she didn't add.

"I'm a good guy. Look, I'm the sheriff. I know things about people in this town, private situations and sadnesses that most folks don't want known. Yours wasn't the only domestic-violence call I've ever answered."

Her hand shook so hard, she put down the milkshake. Sprite nudged the bag, and she handed him an onion ring. His velvet-soft lips nipped it from her hand and he chewed, satisfied.

"I never talk about what happened. Nobody knows. Nobody but you. I think my sisters suspect what happened, but I've never told them."

"How did you explain the surgery and the cast?"

"Stable accident. A horse shied and crushed my

arm against the wall.'' It had been plausible, but that had been one of the only lies, and the last lie, she'd ever told anyone.

What happened with Jerrod had been horrible. It had made her feel bad through and through. But to have lied to cover it up, that had been so much worse.

''I can't talk about this.'' She went to grab her food, but his big hand covered her arm, stopping her.

His palm was warm and the power and strength of him wasn't frightening. It was comforting.

''We don't have to say another word.'' His voice was velvet. It was steel. It was everything strong and everything kind. ''I want you to know I've filed that night away with all the others and locked the door. I did what I could to help you then, and I will now. As a sheriff. As a man.''

''You sound like a campaign slogan.''

''I'm getting the knack of running for office. I *think* that's a bad thing, but I can't seem to help myself.''

At least that cracked the hold sadness had on her. The sorrow eased from her eyes. ''I have been avoiding you. I shouldn't have tried to pretend that I haven't.''

''I figured out why. It's all right.'' He unwrapped his burger. ''We could be friends, you know.''

''Friends? No, I never mix business with anything personal.'' She waved at the little girls riding away from the take-out window, each holding a double-scoop, double-dipped cone.

He chuckled. "Yeah, I notice you never mix business and personal feelings."

"They're little girls. I like kids."

"You could treat me like that. I could wave, and you could wave back. I might say hello, and you might say something friendly back. Think that would be okay?" He waited for her to nod.

But she neither affirmed nor denied as her cell phone rang. He knew it was bad news. It had to be—he could feel it in his gut. He watched her pull the small phone from her back pocket and frown at the screen.

"Colleen?" She listened for a moment. "Thanks. I'll be there as soon as I can."

"Do you need a ride?" He rose, ready to assist her in any way he could.

"No, my best mare is about to become a mom, so I've got to go. My boy will get me there soon enough." There was no mistaking the affection in her voice as she took hold of the gelding's leather bridle.

True love shone in the big horse's brown eyes as he tried to steal another onion ring, and she let him before mounting up with the ease of someone who'd been doing it all her life.

Kendra was a soft touch. As warm and loving a woman as he could ever hope to find. He'd come so close tonight to making this almost a real date. Maybe next time he'd get it right. Hopefully, there would be no emergencies with his work or hers.

A little help, Lord, he prayed, as he handed her the

giant-size foam cup—the huckleberry shake, just like his.

There was no mistaking the warmth in her gaze, in her smile—a small sign, but it was enough for him.

''Thanks for the company.'' She tucked the food bag in the cradle of her lap.

With the milkshake cupped in one hand, the reins in the other, she turned Sprite toward the alley, where she'd come from. She was like rain, soothing and refreshing, on the wind of a needed storm.

He felt the turmoil in his heart, not knowing which way this would fall. He waved and watched her ride between the buildings until she was out of his sight.

He packed up, no sense in eating alone in the parking lot. Probably someone would spot him and come up to him with some problem or another that needed taking care of. And he was off duty tonight. He was dog-tired, he was hopeful and he was defeated all at once.

Alone, he headed the Jeep west toward home. Right before he turned onto the highway he spotted the faint silhouette of woman and horse. Framed by the lavender hue of twilight, she rode into the sunset with her ponytail flying in the breeze.

What hurt in his soul, he couldn't say.

Cameron was in the back of her mind late into the night. The vet stopped by twice to check Willow's progress, and after long hours of walking the mare,

Kendra was grateful to settle her horse into a birthing stall.

A little filly was born in the wee hours of the morning and was sleeping curled up beside her mother, her tummy full and as shiny as a new copper penny.

Even as Kendra climbed to her feet, weary, taking away the bucket of warmed mash she'd fixed for the tired new mother, the image of Cameron kept troubling her. She'd felt aware of him, the way a woman is aware of a man she's interested in, as he'd huddled next to her in the drive-in's parking lot.

The past was troubling her. Her fears were troubling her. It was hard not to forget the stalwart sheriff who'd drawn his gun that rainy night long ago and taken the blow that had been meant for her.

What was she going to do about Cameron? No, more honestly, what was she going to do about her reaction to him? Would she always see the past when she looked at him?

She thought she'd buried those memories well and deep. Yet here they were rising to the surface, haunting her on a beautiful August evening when she was safe on her horse, riding as she always did.

All that she had to be grateful for, so why couldn't she concentrate on those things? It was as if the steel walls around her heart had been penetrated.

She would pray harder, that's what she would do. Ask the good Lord and His angels to help her leave the past where it belonged.

So that when she looked at Cameron now, she

would see the helpful lawman who'd changed her trailer's tire, who owned Warrior, who rented stall number one-fifty-three.

Cameron was the man who'd been perceptive enough to see not the woman who'd been rushed to the hospital that long-ago stormy night but the woman she was today.

If he could do it, then so could she.

Dawn had taken command of the sky, coloring the horizon with reverent mauves and lavender tones that made the hush in the moments before dawn fill her up to the brim. Peace surrounded her from all sides—the rolling fields, the sleeping foothills and the mountains holding up the sky, touched with predawn's light.

She couldn't explain the feeling that washed over her like the first bold curve of light breaking over the giant Bridger Range.

With every step she made on the well-worn path between the stables and her tiny house on the knoll, she felt her life change around her and she couldn't say why. It was as if the path ahead of her shifted.

How could that be? It looked the same to her as it always did.

The horses in their paddocks called to her in turn or watched her pass with friendly gazes. Sprite and Honeybear trailed along beside her, the board fence separating them. Jingles was waiting at the corner post, gazing curiously into the backyard, as if something had caught her interest. As if something was different on this beautiful morning.

The imprints from a man's boots didn't frighten her as she followed the stone walk to the porch. He'd tracked through the spray from the automated sprinklers.

On the top step, an orange furry mound was waiting for her, one eye slit to watch her approach.

If there'd been anything wrong, then the cat would have told her. He was far too calm for there to have been a burglary, uncommon in a town where most people didn't lock their doors. No, Pounce's attitude was more disapproving than anything.

The small self-stick note on the white frame of her screen door did surprise her. The writing was bold, straight up and down without a slope and as confident as the man who'd written it. "Kendra, I let myself into your kitchen. But when you see why, I hope you'll forgive me. Best, Cam."

What did that mean? What had he done? Had she forgotten something at the drive-through? Her cell phone? Her keys? She hadn't taken more than that with her.

The instant she opened the door, she breathed in the scent of warm bacon, sausage and eggs. The sharp comforting scent of coffee. Her coffeemaker was on, still brewing.

The preheat buzzer on the oven beeped. Had she just missed him?

It was as if she could sense him in the room. The change in the atmosphere. The faint scent of his woodsy aftershave. She ought to be mad he'd just walked into her house uninvited, but how could she? He hadn't violated her space, that wasn't the way this felt. It felt, as she opened the oven door, like comfort.

How many mornings had she walked through the back door just like this? Exhausted from a long night sitting up with a sick horse, hers or a boarder's, when the owner would not. Or from welcoming a new foal into the world. Or a dozen other disasters or problems that were all part of her life here.

Every time she'd stumbled into this kitchen, half-ill with exhaustion to measure out fresh grounds into her coffeemaker, she'd prayed for the same thing. That the strong black brew she was making would give her enough kick to make it through a hard morning of feeding animals and cleaning stalls and training and exercising before she could sneak a nap in one of the empty stalls or in the chair in the corner of her office.

She'd rebuilt this cottage from the foundation up, with her own hands and a ton of advice, because she'd had to—it was the only way to afford her dream. She'd measured and hammered and sanded and painted.

She'd hung the cabinets and laid the countertop. Hunted through garage-sale bargains and every relative's attic and basement for furniture to refinish. She'd lived here for five years, almost six, and this had been her house. Never her home.

Until this morning. It felt comforting. Sheltering. Welcoming. How had Cameron done this?

The plate was heaped with a cheese omelette, glistening sausage links and crisp strips of bacon. A stack of well-buttered toast sat on a second plate. It was from one of the restaurants in town, she knew, because she'd ordered this meal many times while she'd met one sister or another in town for breakfast.

Had a man ever been so thoughtful? Kendra couldn't believe it. That he had gone out of his way like that. He must have heard from Colleen about Willow's long labor. Since classes started today, she assumed Cameron and Colleen had been in communication. Maybe even more.

Good. She would be glad for them. If this was the way Cameron treated his friends, then how much more wonderfully would he treat a wife? Colleen had had a lot of hard knocks in her life. She deserved a good, decent man to cherish her.

A warm silken glide around her ankles reminded her that she wasn't alone. She had her cat demanding she feed him, and feed him now, thank-you-very-much. Her beloved horses were at the gate, less than five feet from her kitchen window. Like good old-time friends watching her through the grass, waiting for her to come be with them.

After she fed the cat, she'd take three apples with her plates of food and her cup of coffee and eat on the picnic table out back. With her friends.

She wasn't alone, see what a good life she had? And if so much was missing, the presence of a man in her kitchen, the ring of children playing in the next room, then she refused to dwell on it.

She tucked that longing away with the emptiness where her heart used to be.

Life was what you made of it, right? Her old defenses fell back into place, and her loneliness vanished when she stepped out into the brand-new light of day. She let the sun wash over her as gently as grace.

Her old pony nickered a greeting, the horses already shoving at each other, impatient for their expected apples.

Cameron enjoyed his second cup of coffee as the sun climbed out from behind the granite mountains to cast light and shadow across the roll and draw of the golden valley. If he followed the trail where the sapphire river cut into the valley to the emerald foothills, he'd face the direction where Kendra lived.

Had she found the meal he'd left warming? Was she pleased? Did she understand what he meant by it?

He sipped in the richness of his coffee and leaned against the door of his cruiser. Maybe the mornings he spent alone were numbered.

Feeling as light as those clouds skimming the blue of the sky, he whispered a prayer of hope.

Chapter Nine

"I've got a lesson starting in a few minutes." Kendra left the pitcher of cold sparkling sun tea on the picnic table where her oldest sister and new baby were relaxing.

Allie, a big sister now, played with her baby doll in the shade from the maples and the lilacs. Across the fence, Honeybear was watching the little girl with wistful eyes.

"Hey, Allie." Kendra knelt down beside her niece and held out a carrot freshly pulled from the garden. "Do you want to feed Honeybear?"

Allie stopped the important job of changing her soft-bodied doll to stare at the pony with wide eyes. "No."

"Honeybear likes you. See how he's smiling at you?"

"No."

"Your mommy rode him when she was your age. He loves little girls."

The little girl wasn't convinced. She stood unblinking, watching the pony leaning between the boards in the fence, more interested in having a little girl to adore him than in the carrot Kendra was holding.

"Here, I'll leave this with you." Kendra handed Allie the carrot, which she dropped.

Honeybear looked devastated.

Kendra laughed and ruffled the pony's forelock. "Karen, why don't you convince her? I've got to go."

"Sure, after I'm done feeding Anna." Her sister looked as beautiful as a Madonna, cradling her child, so happy she glowed.

Karen's husband was good to her. Anyone could see that. Through years of marriage and the addition of two children, the love husband and wife shared still seemed to burn with rare luster.

Kendra hurried away and grabbed her hat from the newel-post and headed down the path to the stables before she took that thought one step further.

Ten-year-old Samantha Corey passed her in the aisle, her hair swept back in a French braid. Her cousin Hailey on her black gelding had ridden over from her land just out of town. She greeted both girls, wished them a safe ride and reminded them to stay on the three main trails.

"We're not gonna go out that far," Samantha assured her.

"Yeah, it's too smoky," Hailey added.

The northwestern wind was pulling smoke from the north, where wildfires raged at the border of Glacier National Park. An acrid haze was creeping along the Rockies, hiding their grand peaks from view.

"Everyone is waiting and ready. Lora's with them right now. Oh, there was a last-minute addition and I've got Palouse saddled for you." Pammy Pittman, one of the teenagers she employed as a summertime stable girl, handed over the reins.

"Thanks, kiddo." Kendra took the worn leather straps. "It's just you and me, fella. Is that all right with you?"

The gelding nickered his approval, and Kendra gave him a hug. He'd been the first horse she'd bought for her ranch. He'd been with her from the start and she loved him, this sweet old gentleman who would never be forgotten, not in her stable.

She rode through the arena gate to see five little girls, all grade-school age, sitting in anticipation atop her gentlest stable horses and big, hulking Cameron Durango in jeans and a black T-shirt that read Montana's Finest in fading gray letters.

"Good afternoon, girls. And Sheriff. What are you doing here?"

Cameron flushed as he fidgeted on his saddle. "I'm here to take riding lessons. There's got to be more to this than just sitting here."

The girls giggled.

What was she going to do now? Kendra circled the riders. The horses swished their tails patiently. They'd done this too many times to count. She checked her clipboard. She spotted his name on the last line scribbled in purple ink—Colleen must have registered him. He hadn't opted to take lessons from Colleen, and Kendra wondered about that.

"All right, kids and Sheriff, Lora is the lady that helped you mount up. She's going to demonstrate for us today. See how she's holding the reins?" She started to teach, her words second nature as she wove between the horses, correcting one girl's death grip on the leather straps.

"Am I doing this right, teach?"

If Cameron could make wisecracks, so could she. "You know you are. Are you going to be my troublemaker, Sheriff?"

"Not me. Watch those girls, though. Wolves in sheep's clothing." The corner of his mouth curved as he tried not to chuckle.

"I know a wolf when I see one, mister." She curled her hands over his wrist, not surprised by the heat of his skin. By the hard feel of muscle, tendon and bone. His nearness moved through her like a wave in an ocean, rippling deep to her soul.

"Don't make a fist of your hands. Relax, let the reins lie between your fingers."

"Like this?"

"Exactly. I thought you were going to take private lessons."

"When I called, your employee answered the phone

and told me that you were all booked up for private lessons.''

"Colleen teaches, too.''

"I wanted to learn from you. They say you're the best.'' If pride swelled in his chest when he said that, at least it didn't show.

"Well, I don't know about that, but if you decide to admit that you're as uncomfortable as you look in a class of kids a third of your age, then you can drop out.''

"I'm not a quitter, ma'am.''

"I'm starting to notice that.'' She cast him a bemused look, moving along to check on the others.

So what, he stood nearly two feet taller than any of his fellow students. He was staying put. Kendra was here. It was that simple.

A little awkwardness and feeling out of place was worth it. It was hard to know what would happen between him and Kendra. He'd lived in the dark for so long. Did he have a chance with her?

As if she could feel his question, Kendra glanced over her shoulder at him.

Yep, she liked him. Her look said, "I'm watching you, Sheriff.''

He remembered the good times, before Debra had been diagnosed. The cozy weekend mornings sharing the newspaper and sipping coffee. The welcoming love when he stepped through the door after a long, hard day. To live in the light of his woman's love.

Of Kendra's love. Was that a possibility? Could he find the strength to go through that again? The risk?

What if he didn't? What would he have then? More mornings spent hurrying from his empty house, letting his job fill his days to cover up his loneliness? Of reading the paper alone before church on Sunday mornings?

"Are you doing all right?" Kendra's gloved hand brushed the back of his wrist, a brief, casual touch. Her smile said, "I'm glad you're here."

The bottom of his heart glowed, and he had his answer.

Was it her imagination, or had the hour flown by? Kendra dismissed her class, waited to make sure each little girl had dismounted from the horses, except for the Redmond girl who had her own pony.

Cameron led his big gelding from the arena, trying to catch her eye as she chatted with one of the student's moms and exchanged a few words with Colleen, who was moving in to teach the next class and took Palouse from her to ride.

Friendship. What could be complicated about that? While he waited on the other side of the white board rails, it was as if her soul turned to him like a flower followed the sun, seeking that undeniable brightness.

She needed to thank him. She was afraid to thank him. Why? They were friends now, right? She could walk up to him and say, *Hey, thanks Cameron. That was nice of you.*

Why did she hold back? Her stomach muscles knotted up and she stayed where she was, enduring a mother's natural worry and reassuring the woman that the right training would make her child safer on the back of a horse. All the while, she felt the tangible weight of his gaze and the warmth of his presence like the sun on her face.

She knew the sound of his gait on the earth. Knew the rhythm of his breathing as he approached her, now that the students and mothers had gone and the new class was in session in the ring.

She had her sister and nieces waiting up at the house, but did she want to see them? No, she'd rather let Cameron's shadow shiver over her. She'd rather anticipate seeing his smile.

"I have to give you credit." She spoke before he could. "You toughed it out like a real trooper."

"I told you that I'm no wimp. I'm looking forward to the next class."

"You have perseverance. I have to admire you for that. You really must want to learn to ride."

"Do you think? Did you see all those eight-year-olds?" He felt as tall as the moon. She admired him. That sure made a man feel good. "I think I was at the top of my class, don't you? I outreached everyone. I'm definitely far *ahead* of them."

"Are you trying to make really bad puns? I can't believe this. Mild-mannered, reliable Sheriff Durango has the worst sense of humor in the county."

"Not every man can be perfect."

"Oh, as if any man can come close!"

He loved making her laugh. He stepped closer, breathed in the sweet wildflower scent of her and wondered if her skin was as silken as it looked. "Hey, I resent that. I think I did pretty good for an old man."

"Old? Stop that. In my book, there is no such thing as old. You might want to consider private lessons. I know we can get you on the schedule somewhere."

"With you?"

"Why me?"

"Why not you? Personally, I'm sure Colleen is a nice enough girl, but she's not my type. I don't want to give her the wrong idea." Oh, he wanted to give Kendra the right idea. Now that he was sure of his feelings. Of his future.

"Oh, all right. How can I deny the man who brought me breakfast?"

"You haven't thanked me." He sidled up close, so his elbow brushed hers briefly as he leaned his forearms on the top rail.

"I'm not in the habit of thanking men who break and enter."

"How about if I admit my guilt. I could bribe you to forgive my transgressions. Say another DVD? Maybe a box of popcorn? I could volunteer to help you hold down the couch while you watch the movie."

"You're a noble man."

"Don't I know it. You'll be around at sunset?"

"Show up and find out. Well, my sister's waiting up at the house. I'll see you later."

"Later."

Kendra had said yes. She'd said yes! She liked him. She thought he was funny. She thought he was a man to admire.

A fierce love filled him up until he hurt with it. How could it be so sudden, but there it was, honest and pure and true. Wasn't love a gift from God?

It was what he always believed. All the long nights he couldn't sleep, lonely for Debra, just lonely. All those prayers in the lonesome night, and this was his answer.

He was being given a second chance. At love. At life. *Thank you, Lord. I promise, I won't waste a moment of this gift.*

Emotion wedged tight in his throat as he watched Kendra stroll away, waving her fingers in a dainty goodbye, taking every piece of his heart with her.

Where had the day gone? Kendra emptied the bucket of grain into the feed box in the northern paddock, where she'd built the fence eight feet high to hold the wild horses she rescued. A friend from high school worked in the Bureau of Land Management and called her when there were mustangs in need.

The copper stallion kept his distance. He'd stopped trying to bite her, but he refused to be cordial. He dismissed her as neither dangerous nor useful to him.

He even refused the tasty grain she brought, trying to tempt him into being friends.

The old mare, who bore deep scars across her withers and haunches, claw marks from a cougar, was the bravest of the bunch. What good potential she had. Already sweet-natured and social, she was the one most likely to be gentled. She had a smart, searching gaze.

After she realized the human in their midst brought grain and kind words, the mare waited a few wary yards from the wooden trough.

"Hello, pretty girl." Kendra upended the bucket and the rushing sound of corn and oats tumbling into the wooden feeder frightened all four horses.

The stallion took off at a fast run, neighing at her angrily, circling and tossing his head. The dun mare and foal followed him halfheartedly, not too sure they wanted to leave the grain behind.

The older mare, her black-and-white markings the same as the Indian Ponies that had run wild in this mountain valley and across the plains of Western America, shied a few steps. Scenting good food not to be found in the wild, she waited until Kendra moved a few paces back from the fence before moving cautiously forward to nibble up the sweet grain.

The stallion stayed back, teeth bared but scenting the food. The mare and colt stood indecisive. They'd approach in time. In the meanwhile, the white-tailed deer gathered in the tall grasses at the edge of the paddock, soft brown eyes watchful and ears upright, vigilant but unafraid.

Overhead a hawk circled, calling to its mate, hunting for field mice.

A beautiful evening. Kendra chose a spot, the tinder-dry grasses crackling beneath her riding boots, and sat cross-legged. She could smell autumn in the cooler breeze and in the softening of the blazing sun.

She cracked open her dog-eared paperback and began to read aloud, so the horses would get used to her voice. Used to her presence. See there was no threat.

Hooves thudded on the hard-packed earth behind her. Honeybear's velvety nose tickled the ribbon trim on her shirt. She reached up to stroke the pony's neck.

Sprite and Jingles grazed nearby, the ripping and chomping sounds as comforting as the muted light from the setting sun, as familiar as the sound of her own breathing.

She was surrounded by her best friends. Why did she feel so solitary? The space around her so open? It was a breathtaking evening and she had no one to share it with.

It was oddly comforting how she thought of Cameron every time she felt lonely.

He'd been funny today, so big and tall and out of place in the class of giggling, horse-crazy eight-year-old girls. How that man could make her laugh! Images of how his grin started with the crook in the corner of his mouth and spread across his face. She recalled how he'd teased her…how he'd confessed he wasn't interested in Colleen.

Why did she feel lighter knowing that?

She knew the moment he came into sight on the path between the stables and her house, even though her back was to the cottage. Like an angel's whisper, she heard him. The familiar pad of his gait, how it moved through her like music. She could feel the heavy weight of sadness he always carried. The steely integrity of the man. The zing of joy when he spotted her in the tall golden grass.

When she turned, he stood on the crest of the hill with the garden and cottage framing him, the broad strokes of sunlight cutting around him.

Like a warrior, he stood with shoulders square, both hands on his hips, strong legs planted. The light and shadow played with him, rendering him in silhouette and in the next blink full living color.

When she looked again, it was only Cameron striding toward her in a plain navy Henley and ordinary faded denims. A little of the warrior, of the hero she'd seen, remained, hovering around him like the light.

Her shields dismantled. The emptiness inside her ached like a second-degree burn. Throbbing and stinging and nothing would stop it.

Friends, he'd said. She'd be honored to have a friend like him.

"Isn't this a lovely sight?" His deep baritone rang in harmony with the peaceful night, but the deer took discreet steps backward and melted into the tans and dark golds of the dried grasses and brown earth. "Guess I scared them off."

"The stallion doesn't like you around, either." She watched the stunning animal arch his neck, prancing, snorting as he danced out his challenge. "I haven't named him yet. He's feisty, but he's got a good heart, and he's not terrified of people. My guess is he ran wild next to a farmer's grassland, because he's used to all this. He's curious about me, when I'm not looking."

"He looks ready to take a bite out of me. I sure am glad there's that fence between us."

"And solid, too. I sank the posts myself." Kendra closed her book and stood, sweeping off the bits of dried grass and earth from her jeans.

"Some light reading?"

"Steinbeck's *The Grapes of Wrath*. I always read the classics to the horses."

"They like that better than, say, a good suspense novel? And they tell you this?"

"Yep. Who doesn't enjoy a good story?" The pony tried to grab the book with his teeth, maybe thinking it would taste good. "See?" Laughing, she took the book. "Do you feel up to another lesson tonight?"

"To tell you the truth, my south end's pretty sore from that trotting you made the horses do. The rest of me feels as if I spent time in a blender."

"Well, that's what I was trying to teach you. Posting. You don't just sit like a lump of clay in the saddle. It's work. It's a skill."

"I've had a tough day, teach. I wouldn't mind a nice slow ride, with no trotting and no work."

"What happened?"

"Had a call come in to assist the officer in the next town over. Domestic-violence call, hostage situation. It turned out all right, but a tense situation for everyone involved."

"Oh." The light inside her died. How could she be friends with the man who knew her secret? Who had seen with his own eyes her most shameful moment?

Let it go, Kendra. She stood on her faith like the earth at her feet. The Lord would see her through this.

So why had Cameron come into her life? At first she'd thought it was to help him. Now she wasn't so sure.

"I'm glad everyone is safe," she said, as if he'd been talking about anything but possible violence, and gave Honeybear a hug. "My sister came by today. We're giving my little niece our pony to learn on."

"That sounds generous of you."

"No, Honeybear belongs to the whole family. He's been passed down from my aunt's kids, who learned to ride on him, and then to us girls. We had lots of other horses, of course, but he's always been our favorite. He's the sweetest animal in existence, aren't you, boy?"

The old pony, with gray in his muzzle, leaned lovingly against Kendra's stomach. She rubbed his ears with tender respect.

Cameron's throat closed. He'd never had much of

a family life. And with his mom scraping by to keep a roof over their heads, there was never extra money for things like a pony. "Before my wife got sick, we'd talk about what we wanted for our kids. The things we didn't have growing up. Music lessons and a fancy swing set in the backyard, and land enough for a pony or two."

What could she say? Cameron's loss moved through her, more deep and painful than her own. To have loved and have been loved, to have dreamed and dared to see a future like that, only to have it snatched away… She couldn't imagine the depth of his grief. "You lost your whole life."

"That I did." He obliged Honeybear's gentle request for a chin rub. "Some folks might get real angry at God. Debbie was in her twenties and she fought hard and suffered."

He'd buried the memories because they hurt with an agony that was too powerful for words. How hard Deb had struggled, enduring chemotherapy and radiation treatments that nearly broke her. Her faith had never wavered.

His had come close to buckling. And now he was stronger for it. "God did me a favor, giving me those years with her, and I'm grateful for every one of them. Debbie was good and kind and had a beautiful spirit. Loving her was a rare gift."

A gift? Having to bury a wife didn't sound like a gift. Cameron rubbed his eyes, and in that moment, as the wind gusted and ruffled his short dark hair, she saw deep into the man. With his defenses down and the shadows in his eyes, he was no longer the helpful, friendly, sometimes wisecracking sheriff who protected and served. This man had a tender heart that had loved fiercely. Faithfully. Fully.

Michelle had been right. Cameron was the kind of man who stood tall and loved with his entire soul.

There were men like that? It didn't seem true. It couldn't be possible. Her arm ached, no longer broken, and her soul hurt like spring's first sudden touch. *Lord, don't make me feel this. I want to forget.*

There was no answer on the wind. Nothing changed in the world around her. The season was turning, summer's hold slipping as the dry grasses rustled in the wind and the sun lost its warmth. She shivered, although she wasn't cold.

"Colleen said she'd saddle Warrior for me and leave him inside the back gate. I could sure use a peaceful ride tonight." Cameron strode away, his shadow long on the uneven grass.

Me, too. Brittle, feeling like cracked ice ready to shatter apart with any more pressure, Kendra wrapped her arms around Honeybear. Breathed in the wonderful horsy scent of his warm coat. Felt his comfort in the press of his big body against hers.

The pain remained, tamed into a dull, old ache in the middle of her chest. Arthritic and endless.

She'd ride Sprite tonight, bareback. Too tired to bother with a bridle, she hooked her fingers around the blue nylon cheek strap of his halter and led him through the field and into the stinging rays of the sinking sun.

Cameron was glad for the silence. God's hand was in nature's beauty all around him and it was a comfort. The sweet sap of pine, the sharp scent of earth, the trickle of a runoff creek through a mountain meadow where elk drank and birds took flight.

Kendra stayed beside him. That was good. It was bad. Good because her presence soothed him. She was serenity and peace and goodness, and she didn't even know it. But this love he felt for her scared him. It moved through him like a double-edged blade, cutting so deep to his very core that his entire being felt exposed. Down to the bottom of his soul.

He could feel her within him, as if they were somehow connected. Somehow a part of one another. He felt the raw, wounded places within her heart. In her spirit.

He'd loved Debra with all he had in him. Their marriage had been great. They'd laughed all the time, each put the other first, found comfort in taking care of one another. She had been his world, his entire life. When she died, he had, too, in all the ways that mattered.

He'd never thought he could recover from that black, suffocating grief, but the Good Lord had seen him through it every step of the way. Changing him like a season, healing his heart slowly so that he could live and love again. Cameron had no doubt he was made to love this woman now, at this time and forever.

Did it have to be so powerful? He'd never known a love that tugged at him like a lead wind, consumed him like a wildfire, made him feel wide open and exposed. When Kendra breathed, he did. He swore their hearts beat in rhythm. She opened her mouth to speak and he could feel her words before she said them.

The good Lord hadn't led him to merely a new wife, but more. A soul mate.

Did Kendra feel this, too? Cam couldn't tell as he reined Warrior in, proud that he now knew the right term, and dismounted with a creak of leather. He ached from the balls of his feet to the top of his head.

Now he knew why Kendra was in such good shape. It wasn't only because of the barn work she did. Riding took strength and endurance. Whew, he was sore, and he ran three miles every morning.

Kendra moved like the water, sure and easy and weightless, as she dropped the blue strap of the lead. She hadn't even bothered with bridle or saddle, and left her gelding to graze, his halter strap dangling. Did he do the same?

Kendra answered his unspoken question. "Warrior's trail-trained. He knows not to run off. Come, follow me, there's something I want to show you."

She led the way through the streams of light, the glow from the setting sun casting her in a rose hue, haloing around her. Smoke's haze hid the faces of the granite peaks that were close enough to touch. The meadow was a precipice holding them high, bringing the sky near.

Kendra walked to the edge, ringed by hundreds of wild sunflowers. They brushed her slim ankles, their faces followed the descending sun and looked as if they followed her, too.

When she smiled at him, he took her smaller hand in his.

"You're afraid of heights," she guessed. "It's all right. We're perfectly safe. It's a cliff, but the granite beneath us is thick and solid. It won't give way."

He nodded, unable to speak past the emotion caught in his throat. She'd misunderstood. Did he tell her? How could he find the right words?

His emotions remained tangled in his throat. The power of her touch, the connection that bound his soul to hers, expanded like the twilight, pulsing as if with a life of its own.

He let the brightening hues of sunset speak for him. Crimson seized control of the sky, luring a bold purple to join her in painting the bellies of the nimbus clouds gathering at the southern horizon. The last light blazed in a fiery liquid-red, and it felt as if the pain of his old life was falling away, the last of his grief and loneliness.

With Kendra's hand tucked warm and solid in his, his life changed. The sun sank beneath the jagged-toothed mountains, taking the golden light with it, leaving only the bold-colored clouds and the coming darkness.

"There's Mars," he opened his mouth to say.

"There's Mars," she whispered.

Like minds, he thought. It's more than that. When she sighed, her emotion moved across his soul like the shadows across the sky. The last colors leached from the thunderclouds, drawing the night with them. She withdrew her hand and he let her go, the connection unbroken.

A part of him moved with her as she stood near the edge of the precipice, a shadow and a voice in the night. "Sunflowers are my favorites. They raise their faces to the dawn every morning and look to the sun as it moves across the sky, never wavering. At day's end they watch patiently as the sun sets, heads bowing in prayer. See?"

His throat ached worse, as if razor blades were lodged there, making it impossible to speak.

"They remain patient, waiting through the darkness to lift their faces in worship come the next day's light. I think faith ought to be like that."

"N-never wavering?"

She wrapped her arms around her middle, but she couldn't keep in all the pain. Being with Cameron made the indestructible titanium shields around her heart fall to pieces as if made of tinfoil.

She didn't want to remember. She didn't want to go back, but it didn't matter. Images overtook her, the smell of pizza cooling in its cardboard take-out box, the linoleum floor hard against her forehead, the grit of dirt on the floor from Jerrod's work boots, his hard lean form towering over her, his anger tainting the air like black, suffocating smoke.

Shaking so hard from pain and fear, shaking harder now. The sting from his slap to her face like a burn on her cheek, her ears ringing. She'd raised her arm to block his next blow, but she was powerless to stop his fear. It was like a wildfire, feeding on itself—

Stop. Stop remembering. She wanted to stomp out the memories like a spark in the grass, killing the fire before it could rage out of control and consume everything she'd carefully rebuilt.

I won't let that happen. The memories kept coming. The nausea gripping her stomach. The shocked seconds before the sharp jabbing pain registered. Lord, help me. Please, I don't want to remember.

She didn't want to forget. She'd trusted the wrong man once. She was doing it again. Cameron moved silently. She felt his approach like the breeze ruffling her ponytail. She tensed a nanosecond before his hand cupped the back of her neck.

The warm solid comfort of his touch ripped like newly sharpened steel through her exposed core. The place in her soul she guarded the most.

I won't trust him. She held on tight to that vow. *I will not. No good can come from it.*

"Love is like that. Never wavering." Cameron's touch against her neck strengthened.

"Not in my experience."

"*True* love. If it's not steadfast, if it's not giving and tender, then it isn't true."

His touch sparkled along her skin like the first stars in the night, like hope in a void.

A hope she would not believe in. She sidestepped, slipping away from his comfort. Remembering the man in uniform who took the blow meant for her. Standing over her, as lightning outside the picture window cast him in shadows, knocking Jerrod to the ground in a single maneuver, gun drawn and gleaming as the lightning flared again—

She screwed her eyes shut, refusing to see any other man in Cameron. He may be tender, he may be true, but he was a man of violence.

The stars shone as she turned her back on the view. Trudging away from Cameron as fast as she could go, she tripped on a fallen limb and slipped across stones in the creek. Whistling for Sprite she reached for the horse, who came to her, a warm comfort she could always trust.

"Time to go home, boy." She kicked up, swung her leg over his haunches and settled on his broad back. Sprite lipped her knee, as if sensing her pain and attempting to reassure her.

She felt Cameron's approach, the buoyant buzz of his nearness weighed down by the despair that emanated from his soul. She'd hurt him. She hadn't told him it was her memories that made her walk away—not his wounded heart or his belief in true love.

She led the way through the woods and down the hillside where the darkness gathered. Where loneliness pulsed like a broken bone. The coming storm was swift, stealing the last of the stars from the sky. Rain broke from the sky as she dismounted outside the main stable.

"I'll put up Warrior. Go on home." She kept her back to Cameron and pretended to be busy with her horse, so he wouldn't guess her regret as he walked away, lightning outlining him as he strode through the grounds toward his truck.

The rain chilled her. Wet her to the skin. She remained unmoving until the red glow from his vehicle's taillights vanished in the night and the wind.

Chapter Ten

The banner overhead flapped cheerfully in the breeze as Kendra eased the double baby stroller off the curb and onto the people-filled street.

The first day of the town's annual Harvest Days was in full swing. She had Allie and little Michael all to herself, and a whole day to be a doting aunt ahead of her.

She *should* be happy, for spending time with her niece and nephew was one of her most favorite things. The way she'd treated Cameron remained a dark cloud in her heart, the same way the remnants of last night's storm lingered with a dark promise in the eastern sky.

She'd hardly slept last night. It was easier to blame it on the crashing of thunder that kept her from drifting off and the worry of lightning striking the forests on her land and starting a wildfire.

A chunky toy plane crashed to the street, launched from inside the stroller.

"No!" Michael shouted with glee.

Kendra retrieved the toy and tucked it away. "That's a good arm you have, but let's—"

"One day he might pitch for the Mariners," came a chocolate-rich voice from behind her, as familiar to her as her own.

Cameron. Her spirits soared heaven high and plummeted straight to earth. After the way she'd behaved last night, how could she face him? He'd opened up to her and she'd pushed him away. What was she going to say to him?

"Vanilla latte for you." He handed her one of two tall coffees from her family's coffee shop. "Your grandmother told me how to influence you."

"Influence me to do what?"

"To be forgiving." He knelt, making a face at Michael who laughed. Allie frowned at him, clutching her stuffed pony. "I see the company you keep is improving. You two are sure a better choice than the local sheriff."

"I take any opportunity I can to make full use of my aunt privileges."

"Deb and I never got around to starting a family." Cameron sounded wistful, in the way of an old wrong that could never be righted. "About the time we decided to, she was diagnosed. Guess it wasn't meant to be."

"It's a lot to lose, a future with children in it."

"Guess you know something about that. Can't have a family without getting married first."

"Exactly." Preferring to say nothing more on that painful topic, she deposited a handful of fish-shaped crackers on both trays.

Allie chose one carefully and popped the whole thing into her mouth, beaming like the precious angel she was.

Michael smacked his tray with his beefy little fists and cracker crumbs spewed in every direction. His gleeful laugh usually chased all the shadows from Kendra's heart.

Not this time. The yearning was plain and honest on Cameron's face as he pushed a couple of crackers from the edge of Michael's tray to the center for more fist-bashing. He wanted children.

Her arms felt empty, her life desolate. She dug through her purse for her sunglasses, blinking hard to keep the sun's glare from her eyes. She *wasn't* crying.

"Good punch you've got there." Cameron stood with coffee in hand, wearing a brown leather jacket over his usual T-shirt and jeans. He looked like everything decent and dependable and capable in a man. Everything a good husband and father should be.

She had no right to be noticing that.

Just because Cameron was a truly good man, that didn't mean she had to go falling in love with him. She had a willpower of steel.

What about him? Was there a chance he was falling for her?

No way. Impossible.

Then why did her hand tingle with the memory of last night on the mountain? Her palm had fit snugly against his, a perfect match.

He took the stroller from her as if he had every right to possess it. "I'm an only child, so there are no nieces or nephews for me to spoil."

"You think you can borrow mine?"

"Why not? I'm an accomplished driver. This vehicle has four wheels."

If Cameron kept charming her with his humor, she *was* going to love him. Then what would she do? "You must have better things to do on your day off than to hang around with me."

"I'm not hanging around with you. I happen to be buds with Allie and Michael here. Right, guys?"

"Pony!" Allie shouted, spotting a horse and rider at the edge of the crowd.

"Exactly. My sentiments, too, Allie. Are you ready, Michael? Are you both belted in? Does this thing have a fifth speed?"

"Don't give Michael any ideas. He likes to go fast, just like his father." Why was he doing this? Showing up like this with her favorite coffee, taking over, helping out, acting as if last night hadn't happened. As if she hadn't walked away when he was reaching out to her. "I suppose you're out helping everyone with small children?"

"Sure. Thought I'd start with you first. I've got an election to win."

"That's coming up, isn't it? After this weekend?"

"Yep. This Tuesday. That's why I have to make the best impression I can. Thanks for letting me rub shoulders with you and Michael and Allie. Folks are bound to be impressed."

"You're running unopposed."

"Still, I don't want to get too confident. Put-the-cart-before-the-horses kind of thing."

"You have the job and you know it." He looked so *right* pushing the stroller. He would make some lucky woman a fine husband.

But *not* her. Didn't he know that? He wasn't trying to *date* her, was he? "I have to be honest with you. I think you have the wrong impression of me—"

"Stop." His hand, big and rough and warm, settled on her shoulder. There was strength in his touch. Tenderness. "I have the right impression of you, Kendra Nicole McKaslin."

"And you know my middle name because—"

"Frank got a peek at your license, remember? Don't ever trust him. He blabs. Can't keep anything to himself."

"See? That will teach me never to speed, even fudging it by a few miles per hour."

His chuckle warmed her and wore down her resistance.

"Kendra, would you do me a favor?"

She took a sip of coffee, savoring the vanilla flavoring. "What do you need, Sheriff? Trying to get my vote on Tuesday?"

"Nah, I figure I've already swayed you to my side."

"Hmm, maybe I have a write-in candidate I'm supporting."

"The vanilla latte didn't buy your vote? Then I guess I'll have to treat you to a cinnamon roll, too." He halted the stroller in front of the local bakery's booth. "What do you think, kids? Can I bribe you, too?"

"Bribing? You're spoiling them."

"Just following your example." Cameron ordered enough big gooey rolls to go around plus enough napkins to wipe up the kids afterward and dug in his wallet.

"What's the favor?" she asked, watching him toss a five on the counter.

"Stop worrying about my motives. Got it? I thought you and I agreed to be friends."

"We did, but last night—"

"Last night, I took your hand. Sometimes friends do that. They also step in when the other looks lonely."

Lonely. Cameron was lonely. That's why he'd joined her and the kids this morning.

He stuffed his wallet into his back pocket. "Look at all the families here. Go ahead. Look."

"I don't have to."

"I look at them all the time."

Husbands and wives walking side by side, hand in hand, arm in arm or in that companionable closeness that said, We're together. We're in love. We're a team. Children in strollers or carried on hips or trotting ahead yelling, Daddy, Daddy, can I have some cotton candy? *Please?*

Yeah, she knew. Everywhere she looked she saw what she could never have. Everything she wanted.

Did Cameron feel this way, too?

Kendra accepted the iced cinnamon roll he handed her. The carnival music swelled, lifted by the growing wind. Kids racing by, wind chimes for sale jangling in the next booth and the faint smoke from the fireman's barbecue were all background.

Cameron was front and center to her, the big man he was, down on one knee, handing Allie her miniature-size roll and patiently breaking Michael's into bite-size pieces.

"I suppose you can hang with us," she told him, the shadowed places inside her hurting. "As long as I get some kind of favoritism after you're elected. For helping your image."

"Sure thing. I'll treat you to one of those lattes anytime you want."

"Deal." See? They were friends and only friends. Wasn't that what Cameron meant? He was trying to reassure her, and why did that make her feel even worse?

Allie squealed, pointing. She'd spotted a vendor's booth of stuffed animals.

"All right, little lady. Your wish is my command." He steered the stroller in the direction Allie indicated with both hands reaching. "Hi, Phil. I guess we're gonna need that stuffed pinto pony here in front."

"No, put your wallet away. This is my day, and you're not going to spoil it." Kendra had already whipped out a ten-dollar bill from her back pocket. "And the stuffed helicopter for Michael, please."

A meteorite might have fallen from the sky and smacked him right in the middle of the forehead, that's how Cameron felt, affected as she slipped between him and the counter. So close to him, only air separated them.

If she turned a fraction of an inch, he could slant his mouth over hers in a kiss that would change both their lives. Maybe alter the way she looked at him forever.

Lord, please change Kendra's heart. I'm a patient man, but loneliness is killing me. What he wanted was standing right in front of him. He fought to keep from reaching out. How was it possible to love someone fiercely who didn't love you back?

Or was loving her a lost cause?

"What?" She crooked one thin eyebrow, as if puzzled why he was staring at her openmouthed, like a fish out of water. Or a man struck dumb by love. "Did you want a stuffed helicopter, too?"

"Nah, I'll pass, thanks."

"You look more like the adorable teddy-bear type."

"What?"

"Admit it." Laughter lit her up like the corona on

the sun. With her hair down, rippling in the wind, in a worn denim jacket and jeans, she was unaware of her effect on him. She flicked a few more dollars onto the counter.

"No—" he protested, but it was too late. The vendor was already handing over the little brown bear and Kendra's change.

No macho, gun-toting officer of the law would feel comfortable hauling that around the town streets for everyone to see.

Embarrassed, he yanked a five out of his wallet. "Fair play," he told Kendra before she could protest. "That yellow cat way in the back, it's all yours. And you've got to carry the bear."

"Fine, but lunch is my treat," she spoke up, as if he'd agree to that.

"I could be pretty hungry. I might need two fair burgers. Maybe even three."

"Ooh, and we'll get a big tub of onion rings to share," she agreed, accepting the soft-bodied, striped orange cat. "Thank you, Cameron. For everything."

"My pleasure. This is the best time I've had at a shindig like this in years. Since Deb passed." His throat ached and he turned away, because he was a real man, and real men didn't get sentimental in the middle of a crowd. "I ought to be thanking you."

"Oh, Cameron." As if she could peek into his soul, her eyes filled with a beauty he'd never seen. He could see her soul, too, aching for him. "I'm glad you muscled your way in and stole the kids from me."

"I didn't steal them. I just, uh, took charge. I'm sheriff. The town pays me to do that."

"Sure." As if she didn't believe him for an instant, her hand settled on the back of his right wrist. She squeezed gently, comfort flowing from her heart and into his.

Like a new star bursting to life in a night sky, that's how he felt. As if he'd taken his very first breath, opened his eyes for the first time. A new man, he didn't dare to move as the light, quick brush of her fingers ended and she moved away.

"You can hang with me and the gang for as long as you want. But I warn you, Michael shrieks. Allie cries. Oh—" Laughing, she knelt to break up a fist-fight inside the stroller. A good-natured fight, since no real harm was done.

Cameron knew he was grinning like a fool, but he couldn't help it. Was his cause lost? Hardly. He *was* on the right path. He just had to keep going steady and slow. Show her he was the one man she could trust above all others.

It was his intention to show her that the greatest strength in this world was a man's tenderness.

"Where to next, lovely lady?" he asked, taking charge of the stroller. "Wind chimes or stained glass?"

"Ooh, I have a weakness for stained glass."

"Then follow me." Cameron led the way through the stream of people heading in the opposite direction to the row of booths on the other side of the park. "Look, there's something for you right there."

"The horses." Beautiful mustangs, painstakingly created in colorful glass, dashed along the circumference of a delicate vase. The green Montana prairie rolled beneath their hooves and the brilliant sapphire sky watched over them.

I have to have this. Kendra reached for the fragile piece and plainly saw the one hundred and twenty dollar price tag spinning in the breeze. It was exactly eighty more dollars than she had in her purse.

"It was made for you," Cameron mumbled in her ear, one hand on the stroller, the other fingering the price tag. "Are you going to get it?"

I wish. "Not in my budget. But maybe there's something that is." Beautiful colors sparkled in the sunlight, garnering her attention. She could get something small, maybe something to glitter in her kitchen window. "There, I'll take the hummingbird."

"Not the vase?"

"The hummingbird," Kendra handed over her twenty, complimented the artist on her exquisite work and waited while her blue-and-emerald hummingbird was wrapped in tissue paper. "The parade should be starting soon. Did you want to watch it with me?"

"I sure would."

Why did his smile warm her up inside, the way sunlight blazed through the stained-glass vase?

Maybe she'd kept herself apart from everyone for too long. She'd stopped shining inside—going through her life, pouring everything into her work and into her duties as a sister because she wouldn't get hurt. Not by her work and not from her sisters.

But from everyone else? Distant. Polite, sure, but even in this crowd, she was as lonely as if she was sitting on the back porch on a Friday evening.

Jerrod had taken more than her ability to trust. He'd taken away her will to *live*. She'd been stumbling along, surviving, existing, not living. She hadn't realized it.

Maybe that's why God had brought Cameron into her life. To remind her what she'd been missing, hiding away in her dutiful life. Without making new friends, letting old friendships slip away and allowing work to invade nearly every waking moment of every day.

"Are you all right?" he asked with concern, and she realized she'd been staring off into space.

"I feel almost perfect." For the first time in six years happiness sparkled inside her, bold like noontime sunshine through the glass. Like hope.

And all because of her new friendship with Cameron.

He felt like a man who'd been able to touch heaven for one brief instant. Cameron had the good Lord to thank as he carefully lifted the basket from the passenger seat. Maybe he should have called, made sure Kendra was home.

Nah. He remembered leaving her at her truck after

the parade was finished. He'd asked her if she was in the mood for ice cream. She said she had to get back to the stables and relieve Colleen, who'd wanted to attend the rodeo—an informal annual event to raise money for the volunteer fire department and emergency services.

It was just as well. He'd wanted to kiss her goodbye, but he held back. He had big plans for her, for tonight. He watched her pull away, her pickup joining several of the other vehicles patiently waiting out the traffic congestion in their single-street town. He'd first put in some volunteer time helping over at the rodeo grounds before heading out Kendra's way with his surprise.

He lifted the vase carefully in his free hand and shouldered the vehicle's door closed. Nerves tingled in his gut.

Was he moving too fast? Or too slow? It had been all he'd thought about during the afternoon. Nope— all he'd *worried* about. She'd reached out to him. Laughed with him. Relaxed as the local fire trucks paraded by. The volunteer fireman tossed chocolate gold coins, and he caught a handful for her. With the little tykes there, getting the chance to watch over them, he got a good eyeful of what his future could be.

Would be. He couldn't let fear get the best of him now. He'd come a long way since Deb's passing. He'd crawled through a long night of shadow to stand here in the light of Kendra's affection. It felt like a smile from heaven as he strode through the long rays of the sun that carpeted the path before him.

The path to his new and future love. There wasn't a car in the parking lot, save for his. All the folks were in town enjoying the festivities. It seemed as if the angels were looking out for him—he just might have Kendra all to himself tonight.

There she was, standing in the main aisle of the big stable, a pitchfork in hand. Already he knew the curve of her face, the line of her back, the stretch of her arm as she worked. Tenderness fired through him. It hurt to love again, but he would not back down. He would not be afraid. *I know she's the one, Lord. Maybe you could open her heart, just a little. Help her to look at me in a whole new light.*

As if she felt his presence, the way he could feel hers, her stance tensed. She turned, not in fear, but in expectation, knowing exactly where he stood in the aisle. Like the moon always facing the earth, bound by a great force, she faced him.

"I told you I might be stopping by." As if that force pulled him now, moving him beyond his will, he strode toward her without remembering how he was suddenly in front of her. "I heard it's your birthday tomorrow."

"Heard? Who would have told you something like that? If it was one of my sisters, I'll have to ban her from Monopoly night for at least a month. Maybe more."

"Wow, you're sure tough. I'll have to remember not to get on your bad side."

"Your deputy saw my license. That's how you know."

"Guilty. We lawmen have our ways of getting any information we want." He handed her the flower-filled vase. "Happy birthday a day early, pretty lady."

She gazed up at him with big doe eyes, wide with an emotion he sure hoped was delight. "You picked sunflowers for me?"

"Yep. Look at the vase."

"Cameron." The generous arrangement of sun-flowers had caught her eye at first, but now she saw the delicate-cut glass horses galloping around the breathtaking vase. "No, this is too expensive. This isn't right. I can't accept this."

"Sure you can. I want you to have it."

"But—" And sunflowers, too. Images of last night surrounded her, the nodding flowers, the burning sun-set, how hard she'd held on to her faith. Relying on her belief to help her forget. To keep her standing alone and strong.

"I've got a basket here. Picked up a fried-chicken meal from the café. Even got Jodi to make you up a special birthday cake. A little one, for the two of us. If you want, we can have a picnic, and when night falls we ought to be able to see the fireworks from town. Even brought my telescope if you wanted to stargaze."

She *had* to be misunderstanding. "I've never had a client bring me flowers before, much less dinner."

"I'm a client, sure, but I thought I was more than that."

A slow tremble rocked deep through the scars in her soul. Her ears were buzzing. "We're friends. That's what we agreed on, right? Last night on the trail ride and today at the festival. You and I are just friends."

Why was her voice high and thin? Kendra took a deep breath and let it out. The sunflowers became a yellow-and-amber blur. "We're mostly strangers, Cameron. I don't think this is appropriate. I don't want this."

"I do. I just have to know. Is there a chance that you can love me?"

He stood as stalwart as the Montana mountains at his back, his heart in his hand.

She stumbled back, panic flooding her like a river at spring thaw. There was no way, no possible way. "I thought you understood. I appreciate your business—"

"My *business?* Sure, but last night wasn't business. Not today. Not now. I came here tonight because I thought I had a chance with you. I know what you're thinking. I'm not the best-paid man in these parts, but I'm honest and honorable and I'll treat you better than any man ever has. Or ever will."

"What? A chance with me?" She *couldn't* be hearing him right.

"Being loved by you must be like holding a fistful of heaven. Something a man knows he doesn't deserve by his own right, but by grace. That's what love is, a gift from above. I know. I thought my heart had died right along with Debra, until you came along."

"No, you've misunderstood, Cameron. I'm not in love with you."

He looked crestfallen, but undefeatable. "I know what happened to you. What you're afraid of."

"You don't know anything." There was no way, no possible way, she was looking backward. Only forward. To her future alone. That's the way it had to be. The only way she could keep going. "I won't talk about what happened, and you don't know, or you would never mention it around me."

"Jerrod was one man—"

"Don't you say his name." She thrust the flowers blindly onto the tack shelf and turned, seeing only the haze of sunset through the stable door and the smear of concrete at her feet. She wouldn't allow the past to rise up and drown her. She did not have to remember. She did not have to feel like that ever again.

"Kendra. I'm sorry." Cameron's footsteps pounded behind her, concern raw in his deep voice.

Cameron was a powerful man. He could stop her if he wanted. Hold her captive. Make her feel as defenseless as she had that horrible night and during the quieter, desperate times before that.

The years stripped away and suddenly she was helpless again, on the floor, blood mixing with the tears on her tongue, holding her broken arm to her ribs, curled up and waiting for the next blow to come.

"You're shaking." Cameron's voice sounded a mile away. His hand settled on her shoulder. "You're cold."

"It's the air-conditioning. I'm going outside. Let go of me, Cameron."

"Sure." He released her, looking confused. "You're safe with me. You know that?"

"Sure, you're the sheriff." She didn't think any man was safe, but what was the use of saying that to him? Cameron was a good man, she knew that.

So was Jerrod. Everyone said so. But good didn't mean without flaws. Every human on this earth had faults. Lord knew she had enough of her own, and she'd worked hard on forgiveness, but how could she forget? Every time she was alone with a man, every time she'd tried to date over the years, it was always the same.

She could not help feeling defenseless on that gritty, cold kitchen floor. Terrified and wounded and broken. No man was ever going to make her feel that way again. She'd make sure of it.

"You weren't going to ride Warrior tonight, were you?" she choked out, holding on desperately to the one purpose that had helped her through the days— her business. "I didn't saddle him. I'm going to close up early tonight. Maybe you could go home."

"Kendra." He followed her, climbing through the fence rails after her, radiating concern and strength and mercy, just as he had that night when he saved her from being hit one more time.

Would he follow her all the way to her house? Couldn't he see that it was his goodness she feared? Because it made her want and it made her wish and made her yearn to trust.

She would not run. She would not hide. She faced him, hands fisted, holding herself around the middle, defenses on full alert to protect what remained of her heart. "I can't do this. I can't start *dating* you."

"You say that like I've got the plague or something. Look, I know what this is about. You look at me, and you see him. You think one man hurt you, then any man can."

"I don't want any man. I don't want you. Not like that." She heard the edge in her words. Hated the sound of it. When had she become so hard?

It was too late to take it back. She wouldn't if she could. He had to understand. She had to protect herself. What she hated was having done it badly.

Silence like a startled slap stretched between them as larks whipped through the grasses, skimming on the last light before sunset. Jingles breathed out in an impatient "whoosh" at being ignored.

Goose bumps chilled Kendra's arms as she watched Cameron, a tiny part of her afraid at angering him.

Soldier-strong, as self-controlled and as noble as a warrior of old, he did not move. Long shadows of evening wrapped around him until he looked so alone, it made her want to reach out and pull him close. To kiss the pain away.

How wrong was that? He didn't need her, not really. How could he? He was a man. He was twice as strong as she was. What kind of heart did any man have, anyway? She was right in turning away. Right in leaving him standing there alone in the coming darkness.

She didn't need him. She didn't need anyone.

How long he stood in the field, she didn't know. She told herself she didn't care, but she did. She crunched through the bleached dry grasses toward home, the sunflowers bowing before her as the sun disappeared and darkness came. Fighting the urge to look back and see if he had remained. Or if he had fled.

The phone was ringing in the echoes of her empty kitchen as she burst through the back door. Let it ring, she didn't want to talk to anyone. She felt as if she was breaking apart inside as if it had happened all over again, as if all those years of rebuilding her life and protecting herself had been stripped away, and she was wounded and bleeding from the inside.

"Hey. It's Michelle," came her sister's cheerful voice through the decades-old answering machine. "*Somebody* I know is having a birthday tomorrow. Expect to be stolen away. No I-have-to-work kind of excuses, got it? Mom baked your favorite cake, that's all I'm going to say because it's a surprise, but I know how you can be bribed with chocolate. Be ready at noon, or I'll send the local sheriff to hunt you down! Later!''

The click echoed in her lonely kitchen. *Cameron.* Was he still standing outside? She pulled apart the curtain sheers. Twilight crept across the paddock, hugging the forest on the other side of the fencing. The firs cast shadows over the knoll where Cameron had last stood.

It was too dark to see him. She felt his pain in her soul, as absolute as the encroaching night.

She'd been too harsh, she'd handled the situation badly. Was there any way to fix it? No, if she went out there and spoke to him, apologized for her words and her rejection, it would only make it seem as if she cared.

She couldn't afford to care. Her life was safe. Isolated but safe. That's the way it *had* to be. She couldn't have a good man like Cameron coming around with more on his mind than simple friendship.

But he's hurting. Tears stung behind her eyelids as she sank to the floor. She was hurting, too. Why did her soul ache, longing for his tenderness?

There was no answer as the last shadows of twilight slipped away and left her in total darkness.

Cameron drove without seeing along the two-lane country roads back to the edge of town. Numb, that's what he was. Numb and shocked. He'd left the flowers, but the basket of packed food was on the passenger seat and the smell of fried chicken, normally appetizing, was making his gut twist.

I don't want any man. I don't want you. Her words haunted him. Her fear troubled him more as he slowed down for traffic at the edge of town.

Folks were heading in to catch the last of the rodeo and the firework display. Traffic congestion was a rare thing, but it bugged him mightily as he slowed down to a stall. Hurting bad, he wanted to go home and lick his wounds.

How could he have been so blind? He'd misread everything. Angry at himself, angry at Kendra for not understanding, he jabbed off the CD player. He wasn't in the mood for music, either.

He wasn't really mad at Kendra. He was enraged at Jerrod. What kind of man hurt a woman? Broke her bones? Kicked her when she was huddling on the floor in terror at his feet? How many times had he treated her like that?

Jerrod—the respected state patrolman who'd been captain of the football team his senior year, when Kendra was cheerleader. What a perfect couple they'd made, he remembered. Everyone thought they would marry as soon as Jerrod had finished his training with the state patrol.

How long had he been cruel to her in private? Cameron had his hands full during that time with Debra's sickness and taking care of her. Trying to be all that she needed. But he did remember how flawless Jerrod and Kendra had looked together in public, crossing the street to the diner. How happy her family had seemed with the match. How many years had Kendra said nothing? Maybe she'd feared no one would understand.

Yeah, he'd seen it too many times in his line of work. It saddened him, weighed on his soul.

He flicked up the fan and let the icy blast from the air-conditioning beat across his face.

Some folks who lived close by were walking along the gravel shoulders, and that made the traffic situation worse. He spotted teenagers ambling across the middle of the road. Families bunched together on the shoulder, slowing down the outgoing traffic.

He lowered his window to see if he ought to lend a hand. He spotted John Corey, the volunteer fire chief, heading his way. "Need any help?"

"No, we've got it covered. Say, you're sitting here alone. I thought you might have one of the McKaslin girls in here. Noticed you two have been together lately. Good for you, Cam."

Pain clawed through his chest. He clenched his jaw, refusing to let it show. "She's been a good friend to me."

"Sure, I get it. It's private. I know. You must be meeting her here. I'll keep my nose out of your business."

"How's your wife doing?"

"Alexandra's doing great. She's got the kids with her. I'll be glad when I can finish up here and get back to her."

"Let me take over. I don't have anywhere to be." Cameron had requested this evening off so he could be with Kendra, and that hadn't panned out. He didn't want to be alone. He might as well lend a hand, and this way he could help out John, a good friend.

"What about that pretty lady you're seeing?"

She doesn't want me. He bit back the words. Agony left him speechless as he shrugged. He had to clear his throat. "Don't you worry about me. Let me take over so you can spend time with your wife and kids."

"I'd appreciate it. Joshua is old enough this year to enjoy the fireworks. Cassie is still too little, but I'd sure like to be there with 'em."

"Then go. And take this." Cameron handed over the basket of food, and before John could say a word, nosed his pickup onto the grassland off the road. He'd keep busy, serving his town, helping out. Watching as other men with wives and kids came to enjoy the celebration.

He took the flashlight from John, sent him on to his family and tirelessly worked until the last car was off the road and parked.

Only then did he head home, driving away as bright bursts of red and blue and green lights flared in the sky behind him, glowing in his rearview mirror.

His rental house was dark and lonely as the winds gusted, and clouds snuffed out the last of the starlight. He couldn't face going in tonight. He hadn't realized how loving Kendra had put the spark of life back in him. What was he going to do now?

He sat on the top step and let the night surround him. There was comfort in the cloak of darkness that felt the same color as his soul tonight.

The faint noise from the carnival rides and the stadium's cheering drifted along with the gusty wind. The boom and exploding light of the fireworks blazed up high. Reminded him that everything he'd wanted was gone.

Kendra didn't love him. It didn't sound as if she ever would.

Defeated, utterly alone, he rested his face in his hands.

Chapter Eleven

"**H**ey, who gave you the flowers?" Michelle waded through the grassy field, looking happy and relaxed and lovely in her fashionable summer maternity outfit. "Nice vase, too. Was it from any of the handsome lawmen in this town?"

"Stop teasing, please." Kendra gave her attention to the stallion easing forward to steal the garden-fresh carrot from her palm. "That's a good boy. See? I'm not going to hurt you."

The wild animal retreated, crunching the vegetable, his gaze fastening firmly on her, not ready to trust. But he already was. He just wasn't ready to admit it yet.

The older mare nosed her hand. "Hello, girl. I'm all out of carrots, but I've got one more LifeSavers."

The mare lipped up the treat, crunching gratefully. She'd lived a hard life surviving in the wild, but she was safe now. As if she knew it, the mare hesitated, almost trusting enough to be stroked. Tenderness for the animal filled her. Kendra knew she'd make a fine saddle horse in time, and would appreciate the companionship of the right person.

"You've got them looking pretty tame." Michelle hooked her arms over the rail and squinted, watching the horses. "Even the stallion isn't trying to knock you around."

"I'm charming him with food." At least Michelle wasn't wanting to talk about Cameron. Every time she thought of him, the pain behind her sternum intensified. Then stop thinking about him, Kendra!

"Everyone's up at the house." Michelle ran her hand over the curve of her tummy. "Karen has Allie up on Honeybear. She's having a great time. I haven't seen that old pony have that much sparkle in him for years."

"He misses having a little girl to love."

"Awesome. Only, when my little one is old enough, I get Honeybear next."

"There's still Michael and Allie ahead of your baby." Kendra ducked through the boards, suddenly struck with a grief so large, her knees buckled. She grabbed the fence for balance. She hadn't been this sad since she'd left Jerrod. Or rather, since she'd talked him into leaving her alone.

Being an aunt wasn't enough. She craved a better life. One filled with the happiness and love she saw on her sister's face. Michelle radiated joy, the peaceful, contented kind, and it wasn't only because of the baby she carried safe, beneath her heart.

"Can I ask you something?" Kendra dared to query as they hoofed it up the knoll toward her lonely cottage. "I remember how your first real boyfriend cheated on you."

"It's a small town. Everybody knew but me." Michelle shrugged. "Just like I can guess things weren't as good as they seemed with you and Jerrod."

"How did you know?"

"When you smiled, it never reached your eyes. And there was something cold about Jerrod. I always worried that he wasn't good to you."

"Sometimes it feels as if no man can be." A chill quaked through her. She'd said too much; she could not remember that horrible time, but she had to ask. "How do you know your husband will always be there for you? That you can trust him forever? That he'd never, oh, hurt you."

"Because of the man Brody is inside, down deep. He's a real man, and that means he's noble and honorable and faithful. That his love, when it's true, is forever. Why are you asking? Ooh, you've got it bad for the sheriff, but you're afraid to love again."

"No, I was just wondering. You know how I feel about marriage."

"I know you never dated anyone after you left Jerrod. That says it all, right? Cameron is such a great guy. I won't tease you anymore about it, I promise. I just want you to be happy."

Miserable, Kendra didn't answer. Michelle's words were no encouragement. Ever idealistic, ever romantic, that was Michelle. Kendra had made that mistake once, and she'd vowed to never do it again. Never trust a man who could hurt her, who could reduce her to nothing at all.

Yet Michelle had managed it. Their farm was prospering, their home beautifully refurbished, and Michelle looked truly happy.

You think one man hurt you, then any man can. That's what Cameron had said, when she'd just walked away from him. She'd told him to go home, after he'd been so wonderful. He'd left the flowers behind. If he were a horrible man, even one as smooth as Jerrod and quietly angry, it would be easy. Sending him away would be the absolute right thing.

But he was a good man, and that made it worse. She didn't want a good man. She didn't want any man.

That wasn't the truth, and she couldn't lie to herself any longer. She might wish for that once-in-a-lifetime love with Cameron, but it was simply not meant to be. She wouldn't allow it.

"Happy birthday!" Karen greeted from the fence, where she was holding little Allie's knee, as she was perched on the back of an indulgent Honeybear.

Kirby, sitting alongside her husband, Sam, clapped while little Michael tossed a ball and toddled after it.

As Kendra held the gate for Michelle, she spied her parents on the deck, cooing over baby Anna cradled in Mom's loving arms. One brother-in-law, Zach, lit the barbecue and the other, Brody, tenderly wrapped Michelle in his strong arms. They kissed so sweetly and affectionately that Kendra had to look away.

Not because she was embarrassed, but because she'd never noticed it before—the good men's love that made her sisters happier and their lives better.

Love. It surrounded her, one of God's most precious gifts, and somehow she felt isolated. As if something was missing inside her. Why did she feel alone with her family surrounding her? With their love everywhere?

"Kendra!" Gramma grasped balloon ribbons in one hand as she negotiated through the screen door, her gentleman friend tailing behind.

Just what she needed. Her grandmother's comforting affection, always there, always healing. Kendra wrapped her gramma in a warm hug, so grateful for her. For her family here, today.

She was just being foolish. See? She wasn't alone. She had plenty of love in her life.

"Happy   birthday,   my   dear   granddaughter." Gramma smiled at her boyfriend, who joined them on the porch holding several gaily wrapped presents. "Willard, oh, I see the gift pile right there on the picnic table. Thank you, sweetheart."

"Anytime, dear. Hello Kendra." The regal professor gave her a dignified nod and a warm, grandfatherly smile on his way to deposit the gifts. "Happy birthday."

"Thank you." Kendra liked the way Willard made her grandmother brighten. He clearly made her happy.

"It's too bad Kristin couldn't have made it," Gramma continued. "Seattle isn't that far away. I guess that express package must be from her?"

"Yes. She's the only smart sister I have. The others have been rendered blind by love and have married. It's terrible."

"Yes, isn't it." Gramma laid her left hand on Kendra's arm where the square-cut diamond sparkled on her ring finger. "Shh, I'm not announcing this yet, I'm going to wait to see how long it takes for someone to notice. Looks like the love bug's bitten me but good!"

"Gramma! Congratulations. I can't believe this." Kendra glanced at Willard, who was now supervising, along with Karen, Allie being lead around on Honeybear's back. "Did this happen last night?"

"I'll tell you all later. Right now I want to hear about you. A little birdie told me you've been spending time with our respected sheriff."

"Time, yes. But we're friends. Maybe not even that."

"My dear Kendra, you look so sad."

"It's nothing. Just—" Kendra couldn't say it. It was better to change the subject. "Willard seems like a kind man. I hope he makes you happy."

"He will. I know that for certain. Now, come with me and let's have a look at baby Anna." Gramma's hand on her own was firm and reassuring. "Now, I'm not prying. You know I would never do such a thing."

"Of course not." Kendra rolled her eyes, trying not to laugh.

"I just want to point out that now that you've found a love of your own, I wouldn't mind attending another wedding. Welcoming more great-grandchildren into the world."

Pain seared her like a burn that licked straight to the bone. "What are you talking about? You know I'm an independent kind of girl."

"Fine. Stay in denial, but you can't fool your gramma. Oh, look at how big our baby is getting. Alice, you've held Anna long enough. It's my turn to spoil her."

I'm not in denial. Kendra couldn't believe her grandmother's nerve. There's no possible way. I'm not putting my heart on the line. She'd been down that road and look how it had turned out.

But her sisters had taken the risk…and won.

Zach, done with the grill, had joined Karen by the back gate. They stood together, arm in arm, their love as tangible as the warm sunlight.

Sam had scooped Michael up to swing him in the air like a plane while Kirby watched, laughing with happiness as Sam pulled her against him and they all hugged. Their love as solid as the earth beneath their feet.

Michelle was snuggling in Brody's arms, as they talked softly together. Brody's wide hand spanned his wife's protruding stomach, and they smiled together. Were they wondering if she would have a girl or a boy? Their love for each other was plain to see in their honest affection.

That's what I want. The longing spilled up from her soul before she could stop it. Before she could block it off behind her defensive shields. Too late, the yearning remained a void inside her. An old aching dream that had been shattered, never to be made whole again.

I won't think of Cameron. She fisted her hands, steeled her courage, and still the wish remained. Love surrounded her.

Please, Lord, she prayed, hoping her sorrows would be heard, knowing the need in the world was so much greater than her heartache. But still, she hoped God was listening. *Please make this pain go away. I don't want to hurt anymore.*

The wind changed direction, whispering through the dry blades of grass and the maple trees.

Maybe that was her answer, she thought, determined to ignore the sadness within her that seemed without end.

Cameron had had better days. After a night without much sleep to speak of, he'd put in two long days while folks enjoyed the local harvest festival. Nothing had gone wrong; that wasn't what had him in a bad mood.

It was that nothing felt right. Sunday morning service hadn't brought him peace, as it usually did when he was in need. Peace eluded him. As the calm that came with the onset of evening settled over the town, the businesses closed, the vendor booths packed up and were hauled away; there wasn't a car on the street.

He couldn't put it off any longer. He turned off the lights, locked the door and ambled around back to where his vehicle was parked. Looking as lonesome as he felt in the shade of old maples planted decades before.

Thunderheads chased dry lightning across the sky. Yeah, that's sorta how he felt. Wasn't much in the mood to go home and try to fix something. Even a tuna-fish sandwich, his old standby. Maybe he'd swing by the drive-in.

Everywhere he'd gone today, Kendra had been on his mind. Roaming through the festival, keeping an eye out for trouble, he remembered how he'd spent the day with her. How she'd argued over buying him lunch, but he beat her to it. How right it had felt to have her by his side.

He pulled up to the drive-through menu. "Two bacon double cheeseburgers, onion rings and a huckleberry shake."

His regular order. Kendra had ordered the same meal the day they'd met in the drive-through lane. He'd taken that as a sign. How wrong was that?

"Hi, Cameron." Misty was at the window, ready to hand him back his change from the five he always gave her. "I haven't seen you in a while. I hear you're dating Kendra. She's been keeping you busy in the evenings, huh?''

He winced. This had been happening all day long, and it still hurt intensely. "I'm in the mood for your onion rings. The best anywhere in the whole state.''

"I'm glad you think so. That'll be right up." With a courteous smile, Misty shut the window and disappeared into the kitchen.

Headlights flashed behind him in line. Kendra? No, it was Frank. A dedicated bachelor and a man who didn't cook, he was a frequent patron of the food establishments in town. Cameron returned the wave before accepting the bag of food and the milkshake from Misty, and pulling ahead.

Frank would have joined him inside the restaurant, but Cameron wasn't up for it. Frank would have predicted the outcome. After all, a woman who valued her independence so much obviously didn't need a man to love her.

What was he doing? He was heading north automatically, without thinking, when his house was in the opposite direction. Habit, to drive out to her place. When did he start thinking of her ranch as home? The answer was simple. Kendra was in his soul. He'd never fall out of love with her. So what did he do?

He was clueless. He munched on his burger, still heading north. The random lightning turned serious about the same time his phone rang. Seeing Kendra tonight—and trying to hammer out a solution between them—would have to wait.

If there was a solution to be had. How could Kendra see him and not the past? Could she ever love him with the wounds in her heart?

He didn't know. Helpless, all he could do was leave it in the Lord's hands as he pulled the truck around and headed straight into the storm.

"All settled in for the night?" Kendra asked her beloved mare over the top of the stall gate. Mom and daughter were snuggled together in the clean straw. Willow whickered low in her throat, a gentle, contented sound, while little Rosa slept. "I'll see you in the morning, pretty girl."

The snug feel of the stable was soothing. Kendra took her time ambling down the aisles, where horses drowsed, some waking enough to greet her as she passed by.

Cameron hadn't made it by tonight. Guilt stung like an angry yellow jacket. *I was too harsh. I hurt him. I shouldn't have done that.*

It was too late now. As much as she wanted to explain, it wouldn't change the outcome.

Warrior poked his nose over the gate, sad eyes beseeching.

"You're looking lonely." Kendra stroked his warm velvet nose. "I know, your master is a good man. It's my fault. I scared him off."

There was no choice. She had to talk to him. The last thing she wanted was for Cameron to feel uncomfortable when he was here. With all he'd been through, he deserved the life he was rebuilding. She didn't want him to miss out on time spent with his new best pal.

"You are a good guy, Warrior." She scratched his ears. "Like that, do you?"

The big gelding nodded, leaning closer to give her better access. This was the first evening the sheriff hadn't come to visit his horse.

Longing filled her, sweet and aching. Why was she missing Cameron? He was a friend, that was why. And he'd come to mean more to her than—

No. She wasn't going to follow that train of thought. Heart thumping wildly, adrenaline kicking through her blood, there was no peace to be found.

Not even here in the stable. The past remained like a terrible whisper that would not be silenced. A whisper that followed her into the house, where her sisters were waiting with the Monopoly board set up and big bowls of buttery popcorn and glasses of soda.

A whisper that could not be silenced all through the evening and into the night where she lay, awake in her bed. A fear that followed her into her dreams and turned into nightmares of a man towering over her, his voice a thunderclap of anger, striking her with the fury of lightning while she cried, helpless at his feet.

Dawn came, and with it a cloud of smoke from the nearby forest fire. The dank smoke hid the surrounding mountains and cast a gray pallor over the sky. Like the gloom inside her, it remained, a gray haze that polluted the day.

"I've got next week's schedule figured out."

Kendra startled, realizing she'd been staring off into space again. She grabbed the hose, tested the warmth of the water and sprayed down Amigo. The horse thanked her with a sigh of pleasure as soap bubbles slid off his brown-and-white coat. "Amigo's owner is coming for your advanced class this afternoon. If that's a problem, then I can squeeze in a private lesson for her."

"No, I can do it. Hi, boy." Staying out of the spray, Colleen gave the pinto's nose a scrub. "What about Cameron? He didn't ride his horse over the weekend, did he? Will he be here today?"

"I don't have a clue."

"Really? Tell me he didn't leave those flowers for you. And that vase! I saw them in your office. They're beautiful."

"Cameron is way too generous."

"He's just about right for a courting man." Colleen waggled her eyebrows. "I'd go for it if I were you. He's a catch."

"He's not my type." Firmly, refusing to let the pain swallow her whole, Kendra moved to Amigo's hindquarters, where she hosed down his flanks. "I was wondering if you want to go over the bookkeeping with me later. You said you'd like to learn as much as you can about the business of running a stable."

"That would be awesome. Wait—are you thinking

of cutting back your workload? You know, like your sister Karen did at her coffee shop after she got married?''

"And just who would I marry?"

"None other than our handsome town sheriff.''

"Stop trying to play matchmaker. I think *you* should invite him for a trail ride sometime.''

"Me? No way. Don't try avoiding this one, Kendra. Cameron is a great guy, and anyone can see he's in love with you.''

"He's in *like.*'' It can't be love. She wouldn't let it be.

"Whatever. Here's some free advice. A good man doesn't come along like that every day. If I were you, I'd hold on to this one.''

"I like my life the way it is.''

Colleen looked so sad. "I don't. I don't like going home every evening to an empty apartment. I look at the families who come here and the kids I teach, and I want that. But I'm not going to just settle for the first man who comes along and winks at me. Cameron is the kind of man you keep. There aren't too many out there like him. I don't want you to have regrets.''

I have them every day. Every evening. If there was one thing she could change about her life, it would be to go back in time and never date Jerrod at all. Never fall for the golden boy, town football hero, who'd been so perfect for her, or so everyone said. Nobody had seen the mean streak in Jerrod, and she certainly hadn't until it was too late.

Sure, he'd been good to her. Kind, at first. But over time there were changes. He was strong and brave and upstanding. He was the first person to ever hit her. He would be the last.

Finally alone, she squeezed her eyes shut willing away the memories of Cameron taking Jerrod down to the floor, rolling him over. In control, stronger than the abusive man and just as frightening in his calm, cool anger, he'd snapped the cuffs on Jerrod's wrists.

She'd seen what Cameron was capable of. Of taking down a man as tall as he was, as in shape, as powerful. How did she know he would never use his strength against her? Not only Cameron, but any man?

Why did she still ache to see him? To hear the low rumble of his voice, see the quirk in the left corner of his mouth when he grinned? Why did she feel as if he was a part of her spirit? She watched the parking lot for the first sign of his vehicle. Listened for the sound of his step on the path.

She missed his friendly presence. Friendly, that was all. Was it even possible they could still be friends?

No. She felt the answer soul-deep. It was impossible to go back to the serene companionship between them.

It's more than friendship, a quiet feeling within her whispered.

It *can't* be. She wouldn't let it be.

She felt his approach like the change in the wind, like the clouds skidding across the sun, dampening the brightness. In sudden shadow, she whirled Sprite toward the gate, knowing before she saw that it was him.

He was walking toward the stable, his back to her.

He hadn't stopped to wave. He didn't turn and his shoulders tensed, as if he felt her, too.

Sadness seeped into her soul, but it wasn't only her sadness. It wasn't only her soul.

Chapter Twelve

This was gonna be tough. Cameron had done a lot of soul-searching. He reached the same conclusion each time. He loved Kendra. He was in this for the long haul. He'd stood by Deb in her time of darkness.

A shadow of Kendra's doubt didn't scare him any. What she didn't know was that he was a real man, one who stuck when the going got tough.

The stable girl, who took care of Warrior during the day, handed him the gelding's reins. "I wasn't sure you were coming," she said. "Kendra's already started class."

"Thanks for keeping him ready for me." Work had gotten in the way and delayed him a few minutes, and he'd had to give himself a pep talk on the drive over.

He was sure. He was determined. He was prepared.

Warrior nudged his arm. Wise brown eyes studied him.

"Hey, buddy. I missed you, too." Warmth filled his chest at the horse's affectionate concern. Glad he'd chosen this fine animal, Cameron patted the gelding's neck and mounted up.

Kendra. He spotted her on the far side of the arena. She drew him like flowers to the sun. Hair down, rippling in the breeze, she sat astride her gelding, wearing a pink T-shirt and jeans.

Her lovely face brightened with a smile of encouragement as she coached one of her six little students who swung out of the saddle, touched the ground and sprang back up into place.

Feelings radiated through him, pure and bright and without end. Feelings that ran as deep as love could go.

He'd never felt this strongly for any woman. Not his dear Deb. Nobody.

A soul-deep yearning filled him. Gave him strength for the uncertain path ahead. *Please, Kendra. Just let me love you.* That's all he was asking. To have the chance to show her he would stand by her, protect her and cherish her through her doubt and through every day to come.

"Cameron, we're glad you could make it." She spoke without turning. Crisp and polite, but no more.

He didn't expect an easy road. "Sorry I'm late."

"Just fall in line. We're practicing quick dismounts. Sometimes while we're riding, situations pop up, and we have to be ready." Pleasant, but a very teacherlike demeanor toward him.

Fine. He wasn't discouraged. "Sure thing."

That's the way the rest of the hour went. With Kendra barely glancing at him. She kept her distance, commented on his improved posting skills the way she did with the other students.

He did his best, his palms sweating the entire time. Everything—his future and his heart—was on the line. This would work. He knew it. He just had to hang in there. Refuse to quit. Make her see that he would never waver.

"Our time is up," she announced. "Good job. All of you are working so hard, I think we're ready to take a short trail ride next time."

The class disbanded. The girls broke into twos and threes, riding and chattering excitedly. Cute little things. Cameron tried to hold back his hopes, but he couldn't. Didn't take much of an imagination to see his and Kendra's daughters riding just like that, sweet and precious and giggling as they rode side by side.

Daughters. Tenderness tore him apart. He'd like two girls and two boys. Children to celebrate the pure, ever-burning love he had for Kendra. A wife. A family. It all seemed too close, it surrounded him. They'd have to add on to the house, of course. Maybe an upstairs, make the living room big enough for all of them, and maybe a big-screen TV. Since he was dreaming, he'd make sure he'd add a satellite dish so he could watch Sunday football.

There it was, already formed in his mind. Big comfortable couches facing the TV, a fire burning in the stone hearth, snow falling outside the big windows he'd put in to take advantage of the incredible view. Christmas lights twinkling on a pine tree.

The little girls, with Kendra's beautiful golden hair and blue eyes, playing a board game with their mom. His sons shouting advice and encouragement at the game right along with him. The scent of a roast in the oven, the warm love surrounding them.

God's blessings of love and life and family, everything that mattered. And Kendra for his wife, his love. She would smile lovingly across the room.

"Cameron." Kendra dismounted outside the arena, and the firm line of her soft mouth was anything but loving.

His dream vanished.

"It was a fine lesson today." He'd start with a compliment. Maybe figure out a way to tease a smile from her. "I'm getting used to being the tallest student in the class."

"I'm sorry about the other night. I misunderstood things between us. I thought you wanted only a friendship and nothing more."

Determined, was she? She could push all she wanted, he wasn't going to give in. He would stick. Love was love, it couldn't be broken or dissuaded or stopped. "I scared you."

Her chin shot up. "You didn't. I have a full life, and running this stable takes all my time and energy. I don't have much left over, even for friends."

"Sounds like you're trying to tell me something.

Like you don't want to be friends with me from here on out.''

"That's right." Maybe this was going to be easier than she thought. She'd be honest, he would understand and they could at least be amicable and polite during classes or when they bumped into one another on the trails. "I'm glad you understand why I can never be friends with you, not after this."

"I can't be friends with you, either."

That was exactly what she wanted to hear. The perfect solution. Exactly the best thing for her heart and for her business. Why did his words sound so final? Why did she feel as if she'd lost the best friend she could ever have?

"I don't have friendly feelings for you." Cameron's deep voice rumbled in a way that made her hope. "I have romantic ones. I know you're not ready to hear this, so I'll wait until you are."

"No."

"You need time. Fine. Then as long as it takes for you to see that you can trust me—"

"No." Panic fluttered like a live thing in her chest, and she fought it. Glancing over her shoulder, she realized she wasn't alone with him. But she felt as if she were on the floor at his feet again, ashamed as he knelt to check her injuries. His voice calm and strong, dependable, as he called in an ambulance and she begged him not to. She was fine. That no one could ever know.

"Kendra." Cameron's touch to her jaw, cupping

her face. Tender. Solid. Infinitely comforting. "You didn't deserve how he treated you. You know that, right?"

She nodded, unable to say the words and admit that it had felt that way. That she should have known, should have seen it coming, and she hadn't until it was too late. "Everyone thought so highly of Jerrod."

"I bet they valued you even more." His thumb stroked her cheek, and he gazed at her as if she was the most beautiful woman he'd ever seen.

The shaking deep inside rattled through her, the raw and broken places from that night she'd fought so hard to protect. She'd tried so hard to cover it up so that no one could see what Jerrod had done. He'd taken more than her dignity. Done more than made her helpless. He'd destroyed her ability to love ever again.

How could she admit that to Cameron? With his heart of gold and his integrity like Montana mountains holding up the sky, he wouldn't know, he wouldn't understand. She had to go away. Wanted to run until the pain stopped hurting and her barricades were back in place.

Cameron's touch held her, not confining, but binding all the same. His touch, his love, felt like the most beautiful golden glow she'd ever felt, better than standing on the edge of the mountain with the beaming hues of the setting sun enfolding her. A light she craved with all the broken places in her soul.

And would never deserve.

She turned her chin, breaking away from him. Her

skin tingled, already cold, already missing his gentle touch. Defenses exploded inside her, shields crumpled, she was surprised how calm she sounded as everything within her shattered. "This is hurting. You are hurting me."

"That's not what I want, darlin'. I love you. I'm not going anywhere. I'll back off. I'll be your friend. But I can't change how I feel. Nothing ever will. Like the flowers I gave you, I'll wait patiently until you're ready to love me."

"Don't you understand?" Cold settled in her veins. Pumped in her blood. Chilled the marrow of her bones. "I don't love you."

"Sure you do. A man doesn't marry a woman, stand by her during chemotherapy, do everything for her when she's too weak to do it herself and hold her hand while she dies without learning what love is. What it looks like. What it should be."

"There's no chance." She forced away the image in her mind of him caring for his dying wife, with his quiet strength. "Never. No."

"Don't say it like that. Give it time, Kendra. It's all I'm asking. Time for you to see I'm not like him."

"But you are." Couldn't he see that? "You're a lawman, you're stronger and bigger and you're used to being in charge—"

"Jerrod and I are nothing alike. A real man uses his strength to protect. You ought to know that's who I am. I protect and I serve this community, and a wife, well, I would protect her with everything I am."

"I can't."

"I would protect you. You are a rare woman, kind and loving and like sunshine in my life. I want you. To marry you. To cherish and honor you for the rest of my life."

"Those are words. How can I believe them?" Kendra pushed away, choking, pain like rubble inside her soul. "You say that now, but what about tomorrow? In a year? In ten years? Time changes people—"

"And so that means I'll hurt you one day? That is never gonna happen. People change, sure, times change, but not me. When I love, it's forever. You have no idea how hard this has been opening my heart again. How scared I am that I could get hurt. Lose you. Feel as if the sun has gone down on my world if something should happen to you. I never want to go through that kind of pain again, but do you know why I'm standing here?"

"No, I don't want to know. I want you to go find a nice woman and marry her. Someone who has a whole heart and has enough love to give you—"

"A whole heart? No one on this planet has a heart that is without a scar. Without a broken place. Life is both night and day, light and darkness, and it's a privilege to be here, walking the path the Lord has set before me. Don't make me walk it alone, Kendra. Please."

He held out his hand, his wide palm tanned by the summer in the sun, lined and callused and marked by a ridge of scars, like a deep cut long healed. "Please."

Yes, her soul cried out. She longed to place her hand in his, callused and scarred, too, and to hold on for dear life.

How could she? God hadn't kept her safe that night. How could this man? "Maybe it would be best if you moved your horse to another riding stable."

"No. I won't do it. You can push and push, but you can't change my heart."

"You have to leave. I can't do this. I don't want you. If you're the man you say you are, then you'll respect that."

"I can't walk away." Cameron couldn't believe it. Didn't she understand? His love was like a steel that could never be melted. A light that could never fade. "I'll back off, fine. I'll even get into one of Colleen's classes if it bothers you—"

"No, Cameron." Her words were final, certain. "You have to move Warrior. I'll call Sally over at the Long Horn and make arrangements for you."

"Kendra." He wanted to haul her into his arms and hold her against his heart, take all her pain into him so she could be free. So the shadows would leave her eyes and the wounds vanish from her soul. So she could laugh the way she had at the festival, when their future together had been clear and easy to see. A future together, as man and wife.

He couldn't lose that. His heart was shattering as she walked away from him. As if he were nothing to her at all.

It wasn't true. He felt her love aching within him,

felt her hopelessness and her fear. Was there no chance at all? Lord, how could you have brought me here for no reason?

The only answer was a lifting of the wind, coming hard from the west, rattling the aspens shading the main pathway. Golden leaves drifted to the ground, the first fallen leaves of autumn.

Yep, that's just how he felt. Cameron did the only thing a good man could do. He left.

He never looked back. Not when he reached his Jeep. Not when he pulled out of the parking lot. He didn't look north toward the mountains that rose behind her ranch. He went inside, closed the door behind him and sat in the waning afternoon light. Darkness came and still he sat, his head bowed in despair.

Kendra worked past exhaustion. By the time every stall had been cleaned, every aisle scrubbed, her book-keeping done, every corner swept and every horse cared for, twilight shadows were stealing the daylight. There was a nip in the air, making it too cool to ride. There was nothing left to do. She couldn't put it off anymore.

She didn't want to face the emptiness of the house where no one was there to greet her. Or her footsteps echoing around her as she closed the door and turned the dead bolt. The click of the old light switch grated like fingernails down her spine. Light spilled across the pictures on the walls of her family. She couldn't look away from the wedding portraits or the reminders of Christmases past gathered around the Christmas tree...from the precious captured memories of her newborn nieces and nephew.

She ran her fingertips over the framed snapshot of baby Anna. Gramma's words flashed into her memory. *She looks like you did. That little button nose. That round darling face. That's what your little girl will look like one day.*

I don't get to have kids of my own. No family. No wedding pictures. No Christmases filled with children's laughter and excitement, not in this house.

Her defenses destroyed, her shields nothing but wreckage, she could not hold back the dreams. Dreams she'd buried the next morning, when she'd opened her eyes in the recovery room, groggy and nauseous from the anesthesia. Dreams of little girls and a husband's unwavering love.

Dreams of everything that mattered in life. Everything she could never have.

Not because the Lord hadn't given her the opportunity. He'd led her to a perfectly wonderful man. Who could be better than Cameron? He was everything strong and noble. If she closed her eyes and imagined the perfect man, it would be him.

That's what your little girl will look like one day. The trouble was, her dreams had changed. She wanted Cameron's love. Cameron's children. She wanted Cameron's steadfast love every day of her life.

She'd lost those dreams, too.

A knock at the back door startled her. Swiping at

her eyes, she prayed, *Please, let it be anyone but him.*
She should have uttered another quick prayer, *Please
don't let it be Gramma,* but it was too late. Her grandmother was waving through the glass panes in the old-
fashioned door.

This wasn't going to go well. How could it? It was
hard to fool Gramma.

"What are you doing here, practically in the dark?"
Gramma bustled in and flipped on a few more
switches. Light spilled over the kitchen. "Goodness,
has something happened? Are you all right? Oh, Kendra, you've been crying."

"No, I haven't. Just getting sentimental is all, over
the photos. I need to hang baby Anna's picture."

"I see. Well, where's your hammer?" Gramma set
down her handbag, pushed her red fall of curls behind
her ear and dug through the drawer where Kendra had
pointed.

Just pull it together, Kendra. What she had to do
was pretend nothing was wrong. "Gramma, I can do
that. Why did you drive out all this way?"

Gramma set aside the hammer. "We had a dinner
date, you and me. Remember? My treat. The Sunshine
Café."

"I totally spaced it. I can't believe I did that. I *never*
forget."

"I know, dear. I just wanted to come by and check
on you. I've called and called, and you haven't been
returning your messages."

"I've been busy."

"My precious granddaughter. What is troubling you?" Concerned, she rubbed the wetness from Kendra's cheeks with the pad of her thumb. "Only a man can break a woman's heart like this."

"Only a man, but Gramma, I did the breaking." Baby Anna's picture lay on the table between them. A reminder of what she wanted so much.

How much did she love Cameron? Enough to forge through her pain? To put her past aside forever?

"Gramma? When did you know that Willard was a man you could marry? A man you could trust with your whole heart?"

"Why, that's the easiest question in the world. You know, I've been a widow a long time." Gramma wrapped her in a hug, gentle and sweet, and held on. "I know I can trust Willard completely. That he'll cherish me as I cherish him, because God put him in my heart."

Tears blurred her vision, not tears of pain but of truth. "In your heart?"

"Yes. I can feel Willard's presence before he enters a room I'm standing in. I can feel his thoughts as if they were my own. See his dreams as if he'd taken a photograph to show me. A love like that, so great and true, can only be from God."

That's the way it was between her and Cameron. It was too much to hope, too much to be wrong about. She'd mistaken true love for something else once before. "I suppose a person could just want to love and be in love so badly, they could think that, but be mistaken.''

"God doesn't make mistakes. Only people do.''

"Exactly.'' She felt as hopeless as the coming night. "You can't look into the future and see how things will turn out.''

"Yes, thankfully. Look at me. I never dreamed when Willard asked to share my table that I could be here, wearing his ring, happier than I've ever been. I want to see you happy.''

Had she been happy? No. She'd been content and satisfied. Her life here had been comfortable and at peace. But she loved Cameron, and whenever she was with him, the sky was bigger, the sun brighter.

She was better when he was around. "The happiest I've ever been is with Cameron.''

"Then open your eyes, honey. God is offering you the rare chance in life. I know you're dedicated to making your business a success, but don't be too busy to fall in love.''

"It's already too late.'' She thought miserably of how she'd walked away from Cameron and left him alone.

Whatever chance she'd had with him was gone. She kissed her grandmother on the cheek, made plans for dinner later in the week. Alone, she sank to the top step, waiting, as night deepened.

Deer came close to nibble on the roses peeking through the lattice. The whoosh of Jingles exhaling as she bedded down for the night a few feet away.

Pounce crawled out his cat door and leisurely curled around her ankles.

A few stars popped out as clouds moved, only to disappear again. The soothing feel of night, of her horses nearby, of her cat's company, brought her no peace.

Was there any chance that she could take that leap of faith and love Cameron? And if she could, was it too late?

Yes. She loved him. She wanted nothing more than to know his kiss and to share his life. Yet there was no way. She'd been afraid of getting hurt, but in truth, she'd been the one doing the hurting.

Her heart, like the night, turned cold. She shivered but didn't go inside. This was her world without Cameron.

It would never be the same again.

Chapter Thirteen

"I might as well get this over with." Kendra checked the lock on the tailgate. The big horse inside the trailer shifted his weight, restless. "I'd be nervous, too, getting a new home. Don't worry, big guy. Sally has a nice stall ready and waiting for you."

Warrior swished his tail, as if in protest.

"Yeah, I know how you feel. I don't want you to go, either, but it's out of my hands now." Sally had called first thing, and even though the morning was busy, Kendra needed to do this. She'd started this journey, and now she'd see it through to the end.

If she felt as if she were dying inside, well, no one needed to know that. She was a businesswoman. She would handle this professionally.

After a final check, including the tires, Kendra grabbed her wallet and her cell, answered a few questions for Colleen and headed out.

A quiet morning. Dew darkened the fields, and the earliest leaves were yellowing on the limbs, some showing a deep russet against the sapphire sky and amber meadows.

Kids huddled together in turnouts here and there along the main road to town, with backpacks and lunch boxes, waiting for the school bus. A few little girls from her classes recognized her and waved as she passed.

She waved back.

Odd how seasons changed. So gradual that she'd hardly noticed summer was ending and autumn had arrived in a quiet hush that left no doubt.

Just like her heart.

The main street through town was busy, for a small Montana town, anyway. She had to wait a few minutes while cars turning across the railroad tracks to the elementary school had to line up at the crossing for a passing train. While she sat there with a perfect view of the sheriff's office, she saw a figure move across the front windows. Cameron?

She imagined he was fetching more coffee as he worked at his computer this morning. Where was his cruiser? Maybe Frank was out patrolling the school zone.

The last toot of the freighter's air horn startled her. Traffic eased forward and she put her truck in gear. The deejay on the radio broke in to give the weather report—expect the first frost overnight—and she made a mental note to pick the rest of the squash and to-matoes from her garden.

A strobe of blue-and-red light flashed in her side mirror. A cruiser was behind her. It wasn't Frank. She felt Cameron's presence like an ocean swell inside her, pure tender emotion that hurt as much as it sweet-ened.

She lowered her window, watching in dread in the mirror as Cameron marched toward her as if he were a soldier facing execution. He didn't look happy.

Why would he? He wanted nothing to do with her, after the way she'd treated him. Shame weighed on her weary soul. "Hi, Sheriff. I *know* I wasn't speed-ing."

"Nope." He crunched to a stop in the gravel beside her. "It's more serious than speeding. I haven't checked the law book, but horse stealing used to be a hanging offense in this state."

"Like a hundred years ago, and I'm not stealing your horse."

"Looks that way to me."

Did he have to glare at her with his eyes so cold and hopeless? "I got the call this morning, and I as-sumed you'd approved the transfer. I should have called, but to be honest, I didn't want to talk to you."

"Didn't want to, huh? So, you just stole my horse, instead?" Cameron turned away, controlling his an-ger. She was never going to get it. Never going to understand. "I'd checked into prices at Sally's. I was going to move Warrior if you were going to make me.

I see that you are. You didn't waste any time getting rid of us, did you?''

"You didn't ask Sally to take Warrior?"

"No. I believe *you* were the one. Didn't you call her?''

"I did." Through the haze of another night without sleep and the day of emotional agony, she'd forgotten. First, dinner with her Gramma, and now this. "I'm falling apart. I *never* forget things like that, and now look at me. I'm a mess.''

"Me, too.''

She read the pain in his eyes, stark and deep. An echoing ache throbbed inside her. His pain was hers. She thought of Gramma's words. *I can trust Willard, because God put him in my heart.* And she knew God had put Cameron in hers, because she felt his pain. Bleak and hopeless.

It was impossible. He'd never want her now. God had changed her heart with the same quiet force of summer yielding to autumn, and as leaves swirled with the lazy wind along the empty park, she had to be honest with herself. Every dream that mattered to her was at stake. The rest of her life would depend on how she handled this moment. This last opportunity.

She trusted God with all her soul. If He'd put this bond with Cameron in her heart, then that was a miracle. Didn't all miracles come from love?

Cameron's jaw tensed. "Would you mind stepping out of the vehicle?''

"Sure." Gathering her courage, she stepped down. He held the door for her, a gentleman to his core.

She led the way around the front of her truck to the privacy of the park. Every step felt as if she were marching closer to the edge of a cliff and the earth was crumbling beneath her boots. Would she fall? She didn't know. She could only have faith in God. In Cameron.

He fisted his hands on his hips. "What are we going to do about the horse?"

"A good question." Her fear fell away like an old coat she no longer needed, and the broken places in her were gone. Like dew vanishing with dawn's steady light. "Do you remember the flowers you gave me?"

"The sunflowers? What about 'em?"

"They stand with heads bowed all through the night, waiting for sunrise."

"Yeah. I know about that." Cameron refused to get his hopes up one more time. This was too important. Losing Kendra had hurt too much. He didn't want to come crashing down.

"It's morning. Is there any chance you're still waiting?"

Her question lingered on the wind, and she shivered. It was too late, she knew. She'd been too afraid to believe, and now she'd lost him. It was over, truly. Forever.

Then he cleared his throat. The corner of his mouth

crooked into a grin. "There's every chance in the world."

Joy surged through her, brighter than she'd ever felt. Made more sparkling by the bond connecting them, heart to heart, soul to soul.

"Come here, my love." He opened his arms to fold her close.

She snuggled against his steely chest for the first time. Laid her cheek against his sternum. A sense of rightness surrounded her, the wonder of this man's unshakable love. She'd been alone for so long, and now she'd come home.

"I love you." His confession rumbled through her, and when she met his gaze, she saw the enormity of it, the depth, the power of a good man's love. To protect and cherish and never to hurt.

"I know." She laid her hand over his hand, where she felt the amazing bond of affection that, like the sun in the sky, would light her world for all her days to come. "As I love you."

His kiss was tender and sweet, a warm velvet brush of his lips to hers. Their first kiss. A promise of a lifetime of kisses to come.

"Do me a favor?" He traced her bottom lip with his thumb. "Take my horse back to your stable. Take him home."

"For keeps?"

"Forever."

Cameron's second kiss left no doubt. Theirs was a forever love, forever strong and forever true.

Epilogue

"Good morning, beautiful." Cameron's warm baritone lit Kendra's heart every time she heard him.

Love glowed inside her, soul-deep, as she turned in the chair, balancing her cup of decaf in one hand. The sight of her husband in his flannel pj's, sipping from his steaming mug, was something she'd never get tired of. To think this man was hers to love, this morning and for every morning to come.

"Hey, it's snowing." He kissed her with a hint of passion and settled into the chair at her side.

"The first snowfall of the season." She felt as peaceful as those delicate white flakes floating to rest on the branches of the trees in the forest. "We won't be quite this happy with the weather after we clear the driveway so we can get over to Mom's."

"Baby, my Jeep has four-wheel drive. Nothing is going to keep me away from your mom's cooking."

"It'll be our first Thanksgiving together."

He cupped her chin in his hand. Affection shone in his eyes. "It's already the best one I've had so far. I get to spend it with you."

"As wonderful as this morning is, do you know what can make it better?" She brushed kisses across his fingertips, carefully watching his forehead draw into a frown as he thought. "I took a test this morning. Guess what it said?"

Hope trembled through him. She felt it as his hand gripped her shoulder.

"Are you..." He sputtered and tried again. "Are we...is there going to be..."

"Yes. We're going to have a baby."

With a victorious shout, Cameron abandoned his coffee and swept her onto his lap and into his arms. "I love you," he said, kissing her the way a loving husband should kiss his adoring wife. "What a good life we have."

"Absolutely."

Gramma was right. A love like this, so great and true, could only be a gift from heaven. Kendra wrapped her arms around Cameron's neck and kissed him in return, happy, as she would always be with him in the snug warmth of their little home.

*   *   *   *   *

Kristin is the only McKaslin sister left who hasn't been swept off her feet by true love! But that's all about to change when she finds herself snowbound with a dashing doctor on the way home for the holidays.

Watch for
HOLIDAY HOMECOMING
by Jillian Hart
in October 2004...

a tender Love Inspired tale guaranteed to warm your heart!

Dear Reader,

Thank you for choosing *Almost Heaven*. It has been my pleasure to return to the McKaslin family and tell another sister's story. Kendra aches for a family of her own but believes an earlier tragedy will keep her from trusting a man again. Thankfully, Cameron enters her life, a man as stalwart as the Montana mountains. He teaches her an important lesson: that true love is strong enough to heal any wound and bring us into the light.

Wishing you peace and a life filled with love,

Jillian Hart

TESTED BY FIRE

BY

KATHRYN SPRINGER

Ex-cop John Gabriel was roped into a favor by his former boss—keeping an eye on rookie officer Fiona Kelly, the chief's granddaughter. The fiery redhead wasn't getting department support as she investigated a serial arsonist. But could Fiona's strong faith rub off on the scarred cynic and make him believe in the healing power of love and the Lord?

Don't miss

TESTED BY FIRE

On sale August 2004

Available at your favorite retail outlet.

AUTUMN PROMISES

BY

KATE WELSH

Evan Alton had cut himself off from most of the world, except his children, for years. But when his twin grandbabies needed him, the rancher would do anything, even allow the infuriating Meg Taggert to stay on the ranch to help. Yet caring for the twins brought him and Meg close, and made Evan feel alive for the first time in years. Perhaps the babies weren't the only ones Meg was sent to help....

Don't miss

AUTUMN PROMISES

On sale August 2004

Available at your favorite retail outlet.

LOVE ENOUGH FOR TWO

BY

CYNTHIA RUTLEDGE

Single mom Sierra Summers worked hard to create a loving, stable home for her daughter. Men were not part of the equation—until attorney Matthew Dixon walked into her store with a proposition that threatened her resolve. Neither Sierra nor Matt were thinking marriage, but maybe God had a different path for them....

Don't miss

LOVE ENOUGH FOR TWO

On sale August 2004

Available at your favorite retail outlet.